For *first* and *last* loves, everywhere.

ANCHORED TOGETHER

A Novel

RENEE GARRISON

Sequel to The Anchor Clankers

DocUmeant *Publishing*
244 5th Avenue
Suite G-200
NY, NY 10001
646-233-4366
www.DocUmeantPublishing.com

Published by
DocUmeant Publishing
244 5th Avenue, Suite G-200
NY, NY 10001
646-233-4366

Cover Design by: Babski Creative Studios

Formatted by: Ginger Marks, DocUmeant Designs, www.DocUmeantDesigns.com

Library of Congress: 2020941673

Publisher's Cataloging-In-Publication Data
(Prepared by The Donohue Group, Inc.)

Names: Garrison, Renee, author.

Title: Anchored together : a novel / Renee Garrison.

Description: NY, NY : DocUmeant Publishing, [2020] | "Sequel to The Anchor Clankers." | Interest age level: 012-018. | Summary: "Sixteen-year-old Suzette LeBlanc moved into the Sanford Naval Academy when her father became the school Commandant. She's gaining confidence, but her father's drinking is on the rise, a fact her mother seems to ignore. She finds strength in her friends and finds love with the battalion commander (a.k.a. senior class president) who also must deal with an alcoholic parent. They share their pain, their coping strategies, but can they share a future?"--Provided by publisher.
Identifiers: ISBN 9781950075157
Subjects: LCSH: High school girls--Juvenile fiction. | Children of alcoholics--Juvenile fiction. | Friendship--Juvenile fiction. | Parent and child--Juvenile fiction. | Man-woman relationships--Juvenile fiction. | Boarding schools--Juvenile fiction. | Chick lit, American. | CYAC: High school girls--Fiction. | Children of alcoholics--Fiction. | Friendship--Fiction. | Parent and child--Fiction. | Man-woman relationships--Fiction. | Boarding schools--Fiction.
Classification: LCC PZ7.1.G3764 Ant 2020 | DDC [Fic]--dc23

FOREWORD

If you have a parent who drinks too much, you don't have to live through it alone.

You might be surprised to learn that about eleven million kids in our country are growing up with at least one alcoholic parent. There may be a few in your class right now. And remember, some adults grew up with alcoholic parents, too.

Renee Garrison spent many years denying and hiding the problem in her own family. She wrote this book to let others know that, while they can't control their parent's drinking, they can talk about it. I found this book to be very relatable and deeply meaningful. I hope you do too.

An alcoholic needs help to stop drinking, but no one can be forced to accept the help—no matter how hard you try or what you do. It's also important to know that family members by themselves can't provide the help that an alcoholic needs—they need the help of people trained to treat the disease.

Family members bond and break at different times, which creates challenges in our lives. Families with alcohol or drug problems usually experience a great deal of stress and confusion. Stressful family environments are a risk factor for early substance use, as well as mental and physical health problems.

If someone close to you misuses alcohol or drugs, the first step is to be honest about the problem and to find help for yourself, your family, and your loved one. Talk to someone you trust about the problem. Talk to a teacher, a Scout leader, a coach, or a school counselor. Also, there's a group for kids who have alcoholic parents called "Alateen." Like a club, Alateen has meetings and the kids share tips on how to make life easier. They also have a website with lots of good information. You can even give me a call. We'll find help.

Joe Heagy, Director
Celebrate Recovery/East Lake County
eastlakecountycr@gmail.com
(407) 616-8109

ONE

L ife gets complicated when you're the only girl living in a boys' boarding school.

Suzette stretched across the back seat of her parents' car and scratched the silky ears of her dog, Skipper. Even boys who were terrified to speak to her father, the Commandant, or his family loved his *dog*. The terrier turned out to be a real ice breaker—the perfect excuse for midshipmen to strike up a conversation with her or her mother.

She leaned back into the seat and watched palm trees whizzing past the car window. Hard to believe it was 1972—one year since she moved to the Sanford Naval Academy, a private boys' boarding school in Florida that sounded more impressive than it was. She remembered worrying about so much stuff—leaving her friends in Boston, attending a Catholic high school and finding *new* friends in such a weird place. It seemed silly, now.

She lived among the "Anchor Clankers." At least that's what the local boys called the midshipmen who lived in dorm rooms above her family's apartment. As the only girl who crossed paths daily with hundreds of guys, Suzette understood exactly how a goldfish in a bowl might feel. Since the naval academy didn't allow girls, she was forced to attend Our Lady of Perpetual Guilt, a parochial school across town. She had adjusted to a lot of changes over the last year and finished with an A- average and a few good friends.

Still, Suzette was thrilled to hang up her ugly school uniform for the summer. She hadn't missed the white roll-up sleeve blouse, the ankle socks, or the ugly gray pleated skirt since she left them in a pile on her bedroom floor after the last day of classes. Suzette shuddered when she thought of having to wear them again once school started in August.

"Can you turn up the air conditioning, please? Skipper is panting back here."

Even after a year, she wasn't used to the suffocating summer heat or the mosquitoes, gnats, and an alien species called *no-see-ums* that ate her alive in Florida. She envied her older sister, who stayed in Boston for college and didn't have to deal with the tropical pests.

Today her parents were driving along the shore of Lake Monroe, heading for the turnpike that would take them south to Fort Pierce. It had been two months since the senior class graduated and the empty school building felt depressing over the summer. Suzette missed seeing the midshipmen, so when her friend (and surrogate "big brother") Tim Johnson invited the family to his engagement party, she was delighted. He had been one of her mom's favorite midshipmen — athletically gifted, but academically unmotivated. She knew this weekend would be fun.

After they checked into their hotel and took Skipper for a walk, the family changed clothes for dinner and climbed back into the car. Their invitation was for cocktails at Tim's home, followed by the party at a country club.

When they pulled up, Suzette thought the waterfront residence looked more like a five-star resort, combined with the elegance of a stately southern home. His mother and stepfather welcomed them inside, where whisper-soft shades of blue highlighted the walls and oversized sofas and chairs in pale linen. Suzette put her glass of cola down on a dark wood table, terrified of spilling it. She was glad they left Skipper asleep on the hotel bed. This was definitely not a place where dirty paws or accidents would be welcome.

A gilded mirror glowed on the wall. Suzette admired it, gradually paying more attention to the adults' conversation.

"Then I tried to end it all and, of course, Timmy found me," his mother said.

Wait a minute, whaaat . . . ?

Suzette couldn't believe what she just heard. Her eyes opened as wide as sand dollars and she checked to be sure her mouth hadn't dropped open in shock. Glancing at Tim, who had been sitting and smiling at his mother as she spoke, Suzette noticed the clenched muscles in his jaw. At that moment, the corners of his mouth turned down in a slight grimace.

Her mind raced. *His mother once tried to commit suicide and Tim found her? When was this? How old was he? How awful would that experience be?*

The adults kept chatting and Suzette looked at her father's glass. It was nearly full of Scotch. He had barely touched it, but that wasn't unusual. He behaved pretty well in front of an audience. His drinking got worse when he was at home. Tonight, Suzette wouldn't worry.

Tim caught her eye, raised his eyebrows and nodded toward the front door. She stood as he announced, "Excuse us, everyone. I'm going to show Suzette the dock."

They walked outside to a symphony of frogs croaking in a nearby pond. The scent of Confederate jasmine wafted from a hedge beside the house. She bent to sniff the tiny white flowers and breathed in the sweetest aroma she had ever smelled.

"Sorry, the conversation was getting pretty heavy in there," Tim shook his head. "It really wasn't as bad as you think. We were having dinner one night and my parents were arguing about the divorce."

He stared at the water for a while before he continued. "Mom yelled something like, 'I know how to end all this.' Then she grabbed one of my dad's pistols and ran out of the house."

He closed his eyes as if it might make the memory go away.

"I ran after her, of course," he continued. "She broke down and cried and eventually gave me the gun. I don't even think it was loaded. My dad was drinking a lot back then. But I remember later that night he told me not to worry about my mom. He said that most of the people who *talk* about killing themselves never actually *do* it."

"That's good to know." Suzette wondered if it was actually true. "But it must've been awful for you to worry about your mom."

"Hey, I don't want to be a downer." Tim smiled. "Life is pretty good right now. I've got a great job and I'm getting married. That makes me a lucky guy."

He paused and Suzette raised a hand to shade her eyes from the sun.

"I ran into a former midshipman who graduated from the academy a couple of years ago," he continued. "It was before your dad became commandant. Anyway, this guy was a real jock, captain of the football team, the basketball team, and senior class president, too, I think. All the younger kids looked up to him. He was a big deal, man. He told me he flunked out of college and was painting houses. All he could talk about was the naval academy."

He shook his head.

"It's sad. I think people who believe high school was the greatest only remember their triumphs. They were the sports heroes, dated cheerleaders, and had everything they wanted. Eventually, they grew up and landed in the real world where no one knew anything about them. Their professors or bosses and coworkers didn't give a shit that they'd scored the winning touchdown or were voted class president. The real world is one big disappointment to them."

He turned to Suzette and grinned. "That's not going to happen to us, right?"

The next morning, Suzette and her parents met Tim and his fiancée on the dock. She thought it was kind of funny that he could hardly wait to show off the expensive ski boat his dad had given him for graduation. Suzette figured that was one of the perks of divorce — parents competing for their kids' love with extravagant gifts.

"All right Ski Queen, are you ready to walk on water?" He grinned.

"Umm, why don't you show me how?" Suzette was annoyed at his cockiness, his obvious athletic ability, and his years of experience on the water. Maybe it was good she didn't have a *real* brother after all. Tim was the closest thing to it, and he could be pretty annoying.

She was nervous because she couldn't wear her glasses or contact lenses in the water, so she couldn't see anyone in the boat very well. The roar of the engine made it hard to hear them, too.

Her father slid behind the wheel of the boat as Tim buckled his life jacket.

"I'll yell, '*Hit it*' when I'm ready, Sir."

The Captain adjusted his sunglasses, gripped the ship's wheel and grinned at his wife. Suzette marveled at how her mother never had a hair out of place. Pale blonde locks swept dramatically away from her face and were woven into an immaculate chignon on the back of her head. Today, she had tied a scarf under her chin and expertly applied Merle Norman Frosted Coral lipstick to her lips. Suzette was pretty sure the woman would look just as perfect when she stepped *off* the boat as when she stepped *onto* it.

"You two ladies can be my spotters," the Captain said. "Let me know if Tim falls."

Like that's ever going to happen. Suzette had watched him ski many times.

Tim stood in shallow water and hopped onto a slalom ski at the exact moment the tow rope became taut. Gliding effortlessly across the water, he crossed the boat wake, back and forth, in fluid movements.

He probably learned to ski before he learned to walk.

After the boat made a large circle, Tim let go of the rope and slowly began to sink. Effortlessly, he swam to the stern, as the boat idled, handed the slalom ski over the rail to her father, and climbed aboard.

Next, it was Suzette's turn.

"It helps to wet the skis before putting them on because it makes them easier to slide on your feet," Tim explained as he adjusted the black rubber guard to a smaller size. "It should feel tight, so it might take a little wiggling to get your feet in all the way."

Suzette pulled the rubber boot over her foot but when she bent over, the life jacket slid up to her nose, obstructing her view.

"Guess we better tighten that jacket, too," Tim laughed.

Suzette swung her legs over the side of the boat and slipped into the water. It was warmer on the surface than the bottom, where her toes were. Slimy weeds brushed her ankles and salty water splashed in her mouth.

"Hold the handle with your hands next to each other. Both palms should be facing down, and the rope should be between the tips of your skis."

Easier said than done. Things float in different directions once in the water.

"The most important thing is the boat will start from zero very quickly and that helps you get up on the skis smoothly."

Now Suzette was *really* nervous. She didn't like the sound of the word "*quickly.*" She had attempted to waterski before but never quite mastered standing up on skis. She would have been even more terrified if she was with a real *guy*, but this was just Tim.

"Keep your arms out straight," he hollered. "Don't bend your elbows."

Mom smiled and waved as Tim hit the throttle. Suzette lurched forward, over the skis and hit the water face first. Her lifejacket lodged up around her ears, taking her bikini top with it. She tried to yank them both down when she noticed her skis floating upside-down in the water.

Tim circled around and turned off the motor when the boat approached Suzette. He let the boat's momentum bring it alongside her.

"Next time, let the life jacket keep you floating on top of the water and just lean back."

Suzette nodded. When she was in position again, the Captain gave a thumbs-up and the boat accelerated. She held on as long as she could, until her skis careened in opposite directions and the tow rope handle slipped out of her hands.

"You have to let the boat pull you out of the water," Tim suggested. "When you try to pull *yourself* up out of the water, you lose your balance."

She had heard this advice before, of course, during several failed attempts to waterski. It sounded simple, but Suzette struggled to get her two skis pointing skyward because her feet kept drifting apart. Whenever they got close together, the skis crossed over each other. Even the smallest wave seemed to push them out of control.

"There shouldn't be any slack in the rope, or when the boat starts, it will jerk you forward and cause you to fall," Tim cautioned. "When I see the rope is tight in your hands, I'll go slow and drag you for a few seconds before I hit the gas."

Wet hair covered her face as she was dragged along behind the boat. Suzette held onto the rope and heard the word "*Ready?*" before she was airborne. It felt fantastic until her right ski skidded over the boat's wake. At full speed she landed in a perfect split — forcing her bikini bottom into a painful wedgie.

"If you try to cross the wake with one ski at a time, you'll fall," Tim shook his head. "And if you go too slowly, you'll fall."

On a positive note, doing a split at cheerleading practice should be a piece of cake after this. Suzette's leg muscles began to twitch weirdly after six attempts.

"Shall we try this again, some other time?" she asked, pushing the floating skis toward the boat ladder. Mom looked relieved.

"You had enough, Ski Queen?"

As his fiancée reached down and grabbed Suzette's arm to hoist her into the boat, her diamond engagement ring flashed in the sun. Out of breath, Suzette collapsed in her seat just as another ski boat pulled alongside them.

Tim looked up and grinned. "Hey John, how's it going?"

John Elliott, the incoming Battalion Commander and a senior at the naval academy, waved and cut his engine. Like Tim, John's family lived in Vero Beach and occasionally Tim gave him a ride home for holidays.

"Pretty good, Tim. Captain LeBlanc, it's nice to see you and Mrs. LeBlanc. I heard you would be in town for the weekend."

Suzette peered from beneath her wind-knotted hair and squinted at the boat. John's hair was longer than she remembered, and he wasn't wearing his glasses. Instead of the gray uniform, he wore slightly frayed denim cutoffs, which made his tanned chest and legs look even darker.

Unfortunately, a girl stood next to him in the boat and Suzette heard the name, Jill. She was wearing an over-sized T-shirt—probably one of John's—but underneath it appeared to be the outline of a pretty decent figure.

"And you remember our daughter, Suzette?"

John waved and Suzette nodded weakly, pulling the wet towel tighter around herself. Oh God, her hair looked frightening. She hoped there wasn't any seaweed sticking out of it.

Why didn't I remember to put on a baseball cap? As the other boat sped off, she found herself staring at its wake and feeling a little annoyed . . . or was it . . . *jealous?* There wasn't anything to be jealous about. Okay, so there was definitely more to John than she had first thought. He wasn't just some military geek-turned-battalion-commander. He looked pretty normal out of his uniform. Maybe even better than normal. When classes started and he returned to the naval academy next month, she definitely wanted to get to know him better.

TWO

Florida kids go back to school in August, a swelter-
ing month that feels as hot as the Fourth of July.
For that reason, Suzette was grateful whenever her
mother drove to Our Lady of Perpetual Guilt in Orlando
to pick her up at the end of the school day. It felt so much
better to ride home in an air-conditioned car than to
spend an hour sweating on a slow-moving school bus.

Mom parked in front of the naval academy in her
reserved spot and walked through the school lobby — the
Quarterdeck — on the way to the family's apartment.
Looking around, Suzette found it hilarious that the gray
fabric of the midshipmen's pants perfectly matched
the gray, pleated, Catholic school uniform that she was
forced to wear. *Misery loves company, I guess.*

"Mrs. LeBlanc!"

Her mother stopped to speak to a midshipman who
had red hair and freckles.

The delay exasperated Suzette whose white blouse still
stuck to her back despite the air-conditioned ride home.
She just wanted to get out of her school uniform, fling

herself into the shower, and head to cheerleading practice. She didn't want to deal with a bunch of guys who
followed her mother around like stray puppies, always
interrupting and begging for attention.

Mom put a hand on her daughter's shoulder and asked,
"Suzette, do you know Gary?"

"Umm, no I don't think so. Hi."

Can we speed this up, please? She sighed and shifted her
books to her other hip, ready to bolt. Gary apparently
loved dogs and spent every opportunity playing with
Skipper whenever Mom took her pet out for a walk.
Gary struck Suzette as a real suck-up.

"I hear y'all went to visit Tim Johnson last weekend."

Her mother answered with a glowing account of their
trip but that's just the way she was, a positive, glass-half-
full type of person. However, Suzette barely heard what
her mother said because she spotted the battalion commander walking straight toward her and grinned, despite
her best effort to stay cool.

"Hello, there," Suzette said.

"It was cool running into you in Vero last weekend,"
John said, looking directly at her. "I heard the engagement party was a real blast."

"Yeah, of course I went with my *parents*." She rolled
her eyes.

John turned to her mother. "Hello, Mrs. LeBlanc."

Suzette noticed how different John looked in his uniform and glasses. The deep tan she admired in the boat
was covered by a starched gray shirt and his hair was cut
shorter and neatly combed in a military style. She also
was vaguely aware of Gary standing beside her, staring
and smiling idiotically.

"How do you two know each other?" Gary nodded
towards John.

"Well, I don't exactly *know* Suzette, but I know she can't ski," John said.

Suzette blushed and explained the unsuccessful attempts to teach her how to water ski.

"It takes some time to get the hang of it." John eyes crinkled into a smile before he turned to Gary. "Well, partner, are you ready?"

"I guess so."

Gary was still staring at Suzette as he answered. "We've got a science project on a rocket simulator due tomorrow, but John is handling the illustrations and models because he's a much better artist than I am."

"Gary is very good at science-speak, so he handles the writing part," John added.

"Well, good luck with that." *Great, this will be another excuse for guys to knock on our door and ask Mom for milk jugs, coffee cans, or laundry detergent to use in their science projects. Lucky us.*

As she and her mother walked down the hall to their apartment, Suzette considered her situation like a geometry problem—logically.

I want to get to know John, better, but his friend, Gary, gives me the creeps. Maybe some kind of three-musketeer-thing might work out.

Inside her room, Suzette dropped her books on the bed and did a little happy dance. *It's worth a try. What do I have to lose?*

Getting back into the rhythm of cheerleading practice had been harder than Suzette thought. After a few months without exercising, her jumps weren't as high and her leg muscles felt stiff. She regretted being so lazy over the summer but luckily, four new girls on the squad were struggling, too.

"We all probably need to spend more time stretching and warming up," Suzette told the co-captain. "Oh, and I forgot to tell you I've got the sweater you left at practice last week. If you walk over to my house, I'll give it to you.

The girls left the gym and headed across the street to the family's apartment. It was almost dinner time, but Suzette hadn't expected to run into the Captain, who was already out of uniform and holding a drink. She knew from the red flush on his face that it wasn't his first.

"Good evening, ladies," he slurred.

"Hello Captain LeBlanc," Angie chirped. "Nice to see you again."

Suzette kept walking toward her room, but the Captain followed.

"Are we going to have a successful season this year," he asked. Then he stumbled over Skipper, spilling his drink. He started to curse as the dog cowered.

Miraculously, Mom appeared from the kitchen and took the Captain's arm. "I'll clean this up, dear. Why don't you go sit down?"

She smiled at the girls and steered her husband to his leather recliner.

"Your dad is a real panic." The other cheerleader was laughing, but Suzette didn't think it was funny. She felt mortified as she walked the girl out to her car.

At least when I go to college, no one will meet my parents and life will get easier.

Returning to The Quarterdeck, Suzette dawdled — in no hurry to go back to the apartment. She ran into Dougie, a midshipman who was the same age as she was, although his small frame made him look a lot younger. Many of the other boys teased Dougie about getting

into the movies for the price of a twelve-and-under kids'
ticket. She remembered the night he got stuck in the
ductwork above her bathroom, last year. Some older
boys had forced him to sneak down with a camera to
get photos of the commandant's daughter in the shower.
Fortunately, she heard him first.

"Hey there," Dougie said with a shy smile.

"Congratulations on surviving to sophomore status,"
Suzette said. "I bet it feels good to have a whole class of
freshmen midshipmen starting below you."

"Yeah," he nodded. "It does. How's life at the convent?

Suzette laughed. "Off to a great start. I've got two
projects due next week, including one on finding a
universal definition of spirituality. I guess I'll have to go
to the library because I know zero about it."

Dougie raised his eyebrows. "I might be able to help
you out. I've got a couple of books in my room about
spirituality."

Seeing Suzette's puzzled expression, he shrugged. "My
parents are extremely religious — church every Sunday.
They packed a lot of reading material for me — not that
I'll ever use it. C'mon up to my room and I'll dig through
the stuff in my trunk until I find it."

"Women aren't allowed above decks," Suzette stopped
in her tracks.

"So? You're not a *woman*," Dougie said, over his shoulder. "Hurry up. My door is right at the top of the stairs."

She glanced at her father's office and noticed that it
remained empty — no faculty and no secretaries in sight.
Suzette took the wooden steps two at a time and was
relieved to see the corridor was clear when she reached
the second floor. She found Dougie rifling through a
large metal trunk at the foot of his bunk, scattering
books on the floor.

Suzette stood with her back against the dorm door, but instinctively turned to open it when she heard a knock.

"Hey Dougie, my fake I.D. worked! Let's celebrate."

She heard the sound of a pop top on a can and felt a chilly mist spray over her. Foam dripped from the end of Suzette's nose and landed on her T-shirt, which was enough to make her reek of beer.

Dougie sat frozen on the floor, too horrified to move, while two midshipmen stood in the doorway, clutching aluminum cans.

"Shit, I am so sorry. Oh no. Oh, my God."

Suzette wiped her face. "Are you guys crazy? What are you doing with beer, for heaven's sake? That's totally illegal, in case you didn't know. I can't walk into my parents' place like this. What am I going to do?"

Dougie grabbed her arm and pulled her toward the bathroom.

"You're going to rinse off."

"Oh, a great idea. And what possible explanation will I have for being soaking wet?"

"Maybe you fell in the swimming pool . . . ?"

Standing in the porcelain tub and arguing with Dougie, Suzette failed to notice another boy turn the nozzle. Hot water from the shower head hit her with such force that she screamed. And then, she screamed again.

"No, stop it, right now. Turn *off* the water," she sputtered.

Seconds later Mike McGrath burst through the door. A senior and the second highest-ranking officer in the school, Big Mac gaped at the scene in the bathroom.

"I heard screams and I . . ."

He was looking at Suzette, who stood dripping wet and furious. The outer edges of his mouth twitched slightly but he fought to keep from laughing. "Um, you know ladies aren't allowed above decks," he said

"No kidding?" she replied. "I can see why."

She turned to Dougie and glared. "Get me a towel."

"You two." Big Mac nodded toward the boys with the dripping beer cans. "Sit down."

He peered into the hallway and closed the door.

"We've got to get you out of here before evening inspection. You can't go down the main stairway because you'll run into some of the faculty."

Dougie scratched his head. "What about the fire escape?"

Big Mac counted the number of doors between Dougie's room and the end of the hallway on his fingers. There were only six.

"It might work."

Big Mac stood with his hand on the doorknob and waited as Suzette toweled off. Her rubber sneakers squeaked along the hardwood floors as she slid between the beer-can boys who surrounded her like an invisibility cloak. When the hallway was clear, he opened the door and stepped out, extending his arms to block the view. At six-feet-four, Big Mac stood taller than most of the senior class and wider, too.

The others scurried toward the fire escape, leaving a watery trail on the wooden floorboards. Big Mac ordered several guys to towel the floor dry before the Captain arrived for evening inspection.

"We'll go down with you," Dougie said. "If anyone is watching from a window, they'll just see our gray uniforms."

Suzette frowned at him.

"And don't worry. I'll bring the religion books by your apartment later," he added.

THREE

Suzette walked Skipper in a grassy strip along the shore of Lake Monroe. She tried to escape from the apartment at the first sound of ice cubes tinkling in her father's highball glass. When he drank, Suzette vacillated between looking at the Captain as a disappointment or as a raging, red-faced enemy. Often the amount of scotch he consumed determined which category he fell into.

I'll never live with anyone who drinks.

Yet she relaxed as she looked at the early evening light glinting on the water, reflecting the pink and purple sky above it. Suzette never tired of watching the sunset.

"Had any more skiing lessons?" Gary asked as he headed toward her.

She jumped. "Uh, no. I don't know anyone with a boat."

"Sure, you do. You know me and I bet I can get you up on skis." Gary was grinning again.

"*You* have a boat?"

"As a matter of fact, I do. A Ski Nautique which is docked at my parents' house in Ormond Beach. You should come over some weekend and we'll go skiing."

Based on the way he emphasized "*Nau-tique*," Suzette figured she was supposed to be impressed. But since she knew even less about boats than she did about water skis, she just nodded.

As she bent to pick up Skipper, she saw John quietly standing behind her. *God, the guy's like Dracula or something. He just materializes out of dust particles.*

"Gary believes he can succeed where others have failed and teach me how to water ski," Suzette said, amused that these guys wanted to get her up on skis.

"Ahhh, is that a guarantee?" asked John.

Suzette loved how deep John's voice sounded. It was a *man's* voice and it gave her goosebumps. She noticed he was holding several envelopes, including a pink one with suspiciously girlish handwriting. Her heart sank — it was probably from Jill, the girl on the boat. Suddenly the idea of spending a Saturday alone on a boat with Gary seemed even more depressing than being at home, so she had to think fast.

"I might need an entire squadron — or at least the Coast Guard — to get me up on skis. You should come, too."

John smiled. "I'm happy to help."

"Great. Maybe I'll invite some of the other cheerleaders, too — girls who already know how to ski."

***

Cafeteria food at Our Lady of Perpetual Guilt would never be considered fine dining. Hot dogs, hamburgers, and French fries were the standard menu. A few girls with bony arms reached for the small bowls of wilted salad and packets of fat-free dressing that sat at the end of the cafeteria line, like an afterthought. Adding to the ambiance was the lady who worked behind the counter, whose face was as red as the square pizza slices she served because of the ninety-degree heat in the kitchen.

"What can I do? He has a girlfriend back home in Vero Beach," Suzette lamented, pulling open a mustard packet to squirt on her hot dog. "Not that it does him much good. I mean, when can he even *see* her? They live hours apart in separate *cities*."

"Let him wait. Let him think you're busy with other stuff. Guys love the chase." Her friend Julie bit into the peanut butter, banana, and marshmallow sandwich she brought in a brown paper bag every day.

"I can do that," Suzette said, thinking it was the most ridiculous thing she'd ever heard.

Julie smiled sweetly, but Suzette realized the smile wasn't for her — it was directed at the football player across the cafeteria.

"Thanks. I mean it, really. I don't have anyone else to talk to about this."

"I know," Julie said. "You practically live in a prison. And you are very welcome."

Suzette liked Julie because the girl was a Navy brat, too. She understood the hardest part of any military move is leaving your *old* friends behind and a close second is meeting *new* ones. Julie had a younger brother and sister, whom she was close to — closer than Suzette felt to her own older sister.

"When you constantly move and your friends keep changing, your relationship with family becomes more important than it is for the average kid," Julie explained.

"Siblings can become your best friends because there's no one else.

"Sometimes I feel the kids here at school resent our lifestyle or they think we're bragging when we talk about all the places we've lived," she added. "They act as though they have absolutely no interest in where we've been or what we were doing before we moved to Orlando. Pretty myopic, if you ask me."

Julie, like Suzette, quickly discovered the group that most frequently reaches out to newcomers is often made up of kids operating on the fringes of teen society. Both girls developed a wariness of girls or guys who were too eager to be their new friends.

"Hey, I caught my mom reading this book last night, *How to Talk to Your Teenager.*" Julie waved her half-eaten sandwich in the air. "What's up with that?"

"Look this way." They heard the rapid clicks of a camera shutter just as Suzette wiped a glob of mustard from her mouth.

"Hey, can you cut out all the yearbook picture taking?" Suzette snapped. "Not every aspect of high school needs to be commemorated."

The last class of the day was cancelled and kids were forced to attend a dress rehearsal of the school play, *The Strange Case of Dr. Jekyll and Mr. Hyde.* Suzette watched intently, thinking that it seemed strangely familiar. All of a sudden it hit her: *Oh my God. This is what it means to be the daughter of a drunk. Sort of like Jekyll and Hyde, my dad morphs from friend to foe. Kind of scary.*

From the outside, she was pretty sure her family looked typical—a mother and father living with their daughter and a dog. But if anyone stepped *inside*, they would find themselves tangled in emotional chaos. She didn't need to watch a drama onstage. She *lived* with it.

FOUR

During the bus ride home all of the windows were down, whipping Suzette's hair into a mass of tangles. She didn't care. It was better than sweating. Big Mac waited in the car with Mom at the bus stop. Surprised, Suzette dropped her books on the back seat and turned the air conditioning vents to blow straight at her.

"Dad's secretary told me about the Cassadaga Spiritualist Camp, a community that started in 1875," Mom gushed. "We have an appointment for a psychic reading."

Suzette figured the Catholic Church probably wouldn't approve of psychics, but she sort of remembered going to a Tea Room in Boston with her mother and grandmother. The women drank their tea without milk and when they finished, a medium turned each cup over to read their fortunes in the leaves.

"A medium is someone who can communicate with people who have died and passed into the spirit world," Mom explained. "It's comforting to those of us left behind who want to hear from our loved ones, like nana and your grandfather. Mediums set their own appointments, and I've already called to arrange one for all of us. You don't have cheerleading practice today, so the timing is perfect. Big Mac even said he wants to come, too."

Suzette scratched at her ankle through her white socks. She was pretty sure they were giving her a rash. Then she settled back into her seat as the car headed for Cassadaga just off Interstate 4 between Sanford and Daytona Beach. Quaint wooden houses stood along curving, hilly roads and many yards included signposts printed with the word *Medium*.

"Looks like a very peaceful place," Big Mac observed.

The captain's secretary had given Mom a brochure and Suzette read it aloud as they drove.

"The Spiritualist Camp was established by George P. Colby for the purpose of being a haven for Spiritualists to practice their beliefs while escaping the cold winters in Cassadaga, New York. Since its founding in 1875, it has been a place where mediums and spiritual healers lived, gave readings, demonstrated public message work, and taught classes."

Earlier in the day her mother called a medium recommended by the secretary, a man who used the title, Reverend. The trio drove slowly through the camp's narrow, dusty streets until they arrived at his small house with white shiplap siding and a tiny screened porch.

A plump, white-haired man wearing a dress shirt and pants with suspenders met them at the door.

He looks so . . . normal. Like somebody's grandpa. Suzette wasn't expecting a pointy wizard's hat and robes, exactly. But something about him should say, *I communicate with the dead.*

"I meet people from all over the world who come to visit our quaint, historical community," the Reverend smiled as he shook Mom's hand. "Cassadaga is even listed on the National Register of Historic Places."

"So, what do we have to do?" Suzette asked.

The Reverend explained. "A reading is when a person's relatives, friends, and Spiritual Guides are "brought through," to prove that life continues after the "physical death" and to offer information or advice from people in the Spirit World. You just sit quietly and I'll tell you what I hear. Then I'll try to answer any questions you may have."

"In a Life Guidance Reading, the information comes primarily from a person's own energy field and Spiritual energies," he added. "It's intended to give someone another kind of insight and guidance, similar to what is thought of as a traditional psychic reading. I particularly enjoy reuniting spirit loved ones and those still on this side of life together for communication and questions."

While her mother went into a small sitting room with the Reverend, Suzette and Big Mac waited for their turn in separate area.

"They probably moved us away from your mom so our 'Spiritual Energies' don't interfere with her psychic reading," he said, grinning.

Suzette leafed through a book on the coffee table and discovered that George P. Colby was a trance medium who traveled to different states, giving readings and seances.

She read that Colby worked with several spirit guides. *"One of his spirit guides was an Indian named Seneca, who appeared to Colby during a seance in Iowa. According to Colby, Seneca had instructed him to travel south to*

Florida, where he eventually arrived at a place called the Blue Springs Landing, near Orange City."

"Wow, it's kind of a weird coincidence that midshipmen from the naval academy like to swim there, too," Suzette said. "The Colby guy first saw Blue Springs during the séance in Iowa and he actually wound up here."

"Very cool," Big Mac replied. "Especially since he probably didn't even have a map."

"It says the people who came to the Spiritualist Camp in the early days were affluent and well-educated," she continued. "Not total nuts or weirdos, so I guess we're safe."

"Good to know," he said. "You know who would love seeing this place? My roommate, John Elliott. He would do a great job sketching this town. He's a talented artist."

"Bring him a brochure. Maybe he can take his girlfriend when she visits."

Big Mac looked puzzled.

"What girlfriend? John doesn't have a girlfriend."

"But I thought . . . I met someone named Jill in Vero Beach."

"I think there was a girl who used to tutor him, but she dates an older, college guy. All I know is there's no girlfriend now."

Just then the door to the sitting room opened and Mom came out, smiling and motioning to Suzette to go inside. The reverend held a chair for her and then settled into an overstuffed armchair on the opposite side of a table decorated with three lighted candles. Suzette noticed the man didn't make eye contact with her, preferring to stare at the space just beyond her left shoulder.

"Be wary of young men who will not have your best interests at heart," he said, cocking his head. "They may invite you to dinner but try to extract a price for it, later. However, I see many young suitors in your life."

I wonder who crossed over and is telling him this? Is John one of those suitors? Do the spirits provide like, a list of names?

A fan hummed in a corner of the room as the reverend continued talking.

"I hear someone playing the piano," he said. "Ahh, your grandmother. She loves you very much. She wants me to tell you to follow your instincts. Don't rely on anyone else for your happiness or self-worth, especially boys. She says you are a smart girl."

"Umm . . . okay. Please tell Nana that I said hi."

He held three fountain pens in his right hand and rolled them as he spoke. Occasionally, he paused and it looked like he was listening to someone.

I wish he could see if the Captain will ever stop drinking. Or if I ever move away from it. But I guess he's not dead, yet, so the spirits don't know.

Thirty minutes later, it was Big Mac's turn. Eventually the three climbed into their car and waved to the reverend, who stood in the doorway and waved back.

"Well, how did your sessions go," Big Mac asked as he turned the car toward the Interstate. Mom always let midshipmen drive whenever she took them anywhere. She thought they needed the practice, since the naval academy didn't permit students to have cars at school.

Big Mac talked about his own reading by the reverend. "He told me 'I see you living under another state flag,' which is true, since I'll be moving back to Connecticut after graduation. But that's not really earth-shattering information."

"Really?" Suzette laughed. "I was told to be careful about boys who buy your dinner and want to get paid for it *later*. Mom, did Nana play the piano?"

"All the time," Mom said. "People loved having her at their parties because everyone would wind up singing along while she played."

During her mother's reading, the reverend saw two wedding rings on her hand.

"Whatever that means," Mom said, shaking her head. "I'm sorry to say the man wasn't too specific."

She touched Suzette's cheek gently with the palm of her hand. "Maybe it's good that we can't see the future. Maybe we wouldn't like knowing about it, after all."

Big Mac parked Mom's car and hurried to his room to get ready for evening formation. Suzette remembered watching all the midshipmen standing at attention for roll call and the lowering of the American flag, which occurred before they raced into the Mess Hall to eat dinner. Her family had joined them a few times and seen the food served family style, which meant lots of hollering to "pass the potatoes" or the "mystery meat."

Still, she kind of envied the chaos of the boys' meals, as she set the dining table in her quiet apartment. Mom cooked a pretty good chicken with rice and peas, but Suzette felt uneasy when she saw the Captain bring a highball glass to the table. When he drank, her father argued with anyone near him. It was a relief when he finished his meal and poured another drink before settling in his recliner in front of the television. Occasionally, boys stopped by in the evening to get Mom's help with a project or visit with Suzette instead of going to study hall. On those nights, she caught Mom glancing down the hall to be sure the Captain didn't hear midshipmen in the house. If he appeared, slurring his words, the boys could gossip.

"We don't want anyone at this school questioning your father's authority," Mom admitted once.

Later as Suzette climbed into bed and clicked off the lamp on her nightstand, she decided that living with a drunk was a lot like walking on eggshells. She never knew what would set him off on a tirade and it totally stressed her out. She coped by trying to be quiet and keep to herself so the Captain wouldn't get argumentative with *her*. Most of the time, it worked.

FIVE

The sun rose in a cloudless sky on Saturday morning, but Mom's mood was anything but sunny.

"I want you to be very careful on the water," she said, biting her lower lip. "Maybe I should call Gary's parents to be sure they're alright with everyone spending the night. I don't recall meeting them at any school function."

"Jeez, Mom, I'll be fine. I know how to swim. And there are five of us going. Like you've always told me, there's safety in numbers."

An hour later, Suzette, John, and two other girls from the cheerleading squad arrived at Gary's home at the beach. His mother waved to them from the front porch.

"We're so glad to have y'all home for a visit." She hugged her son. "I hear you're learning to ski, Suzette. It's took me a while to get the hang of it, too, but don't worry. Cypress Gardens will be calling you to star in their water show real soon."

The girls laughed and followed the boys through the house to the boat dock out back. Gary pulled his shirt off as he cranked the motor. Soon they were skimming the surface of the Halifax River. Suzette enjoyed the warm sun on her shoulders as she pulled her hair into a ponytail and snapped on a life jacket.

Gary slowed the engine to idle and turned to the others. "We're heading into the Tomoka River because the water's a little calmer." He winked at Suzette.

They rode for a few minutes and found a wide bend in the river without any other boaters nearby. Gary turned off the engine and dropped the boat ladder. John slid over the rail as Suzette edged gingerly down the ladder into the water. Even on the hottest day, the water always felt startlingly chilly.

"Gary, if we stay close to shore, I can hold Suzette steady and help her balance," John said.

He turned to Suzette. "You just focus on leaning back on my chest with your knees bent."

Thank you, God.

She didn't wait for a second invitation. Her heart hammered, though she wasn't sure if it was simply terror at the thought of falling or excitement about feeling John's arms around her. The girls clapped and hollered encouragement when she managed to slide both of her feet into the skis as she floated in the water.

"It looks a lot easier when *you* guys do it." She pulled a hunk of wet hair out of her eyes. *Wait a minute, is that seaweed?*

"That's just because we've been doing it longer. You had a lot of waves off the coast of Cape Cod to deal with. The water around Florida is calmer. Unless there's a hurricane, of course."

Once again, Suzette tried to stand on the skis without much success. After being dragged behind the boat — and falling too many times to count, she let go of the tow rope and shouted that she was ready to watch the professionals demonstrate how to do it. It was much more fun to ride in the boat, wrapped in a towel, alerting the driver when a skier fell.

After the other cheerleaders and both boys took their turn skiing behind the boat, Gary motored back to the dock.

Suzette was surprised at how much his parents' home reminded her of her own grandmother's house in Boston. Dark furniture sat on oriental rugs while lacy curtains matched a lace cloth on a dining room table. She noticed the table was set formally, with china plates. Somehow Gary's parents seemed a lot older than her own. Pictures of an older sister who was married (and whose old bedroom the girls were sleeping in) were prominently displayed. Suzette guessed that maybe one reason why Gary and John were such good friends is that they had something in common. They both were the youngest kid in an older family.

His parents were easy to talk to, though, and curious about life at the naval academy. "The midshipmen certainly are lucky to have such pretty Sanford girls as their cheerleaders," Gary's dad said with a chuckle. Suzette noticed that the man didn't have a cocktail.

Must be nice to have a father who only drinks iced tea.

But it made Suzette slightly uncomfortable that his mother barely spoke to anyone else at the dinner table. "How do you like living in Florida after Boston? Where do you go to school? Do you have any brothers or sisters?"

The woman focused on *her* the entire time, but none of the other girls. Suzette guessed it must be because of her father's position at the naval academy rather than anything Gary might have said.

After enjoying a slice of the best carrot cake with cream cheese frosting she had ever eaten, Suzette and the others helped clear the dinner dishes. The phone rang. It was a call from her mom. Gary's mother chatted a while and assured her mother that the kids were in good hands.

"I'm stuffed." Gary patted his stomach. "Is anyone up for taking a ride?"

Assuring his parents they wouldn't be out late, Gary grabbed the keys to the Camaro and flipped the driver's seat forward so Suzette and the girls could climb into the back. There wasn't much space, but she folded her legs up to her chin as they cruised along State Road A1A in Daytona Beach. Somehow the neon signs of T-shirt shops and tattoo parlors looked pretty at night when the dirty sidewalks receded in the dark.

"Suzette, you probably don't know this since you're from Boston, but State Road A1A runs along the Atlantic Ocean," Gary explained. "It starts in Key West at the southern tip of Florida, and goes all the way up to Fernandina Beach, near the Georgia state line. It's the main road through the beach towns on Florida's east coast barrier islands."

"Thanks for the geography lesson," Suzette teased.

"We're heading for a stretch of sand just north of Ormond that's pretty quiet," Gary said. "People don't go there much, because that part of the beach isn't drivable. Let's check out the waves."

"Might even be a nice night for a swim . . ." John said. He looked over his shoulder and grinned as Suzette's eyes widened. From someone that good-looking, even the smallest bit of attention was like the brightest spotlight focused on her.

They parked on an unpaved road and walked across the dunes to the flat, sandy beach. Warm water lapped at their ankles, illuminated by stars and a full moon overhead.

"Ever been skinny dipping?" Gary wiggled his eyebrows.

No. Have you ever been in the Atlantic Ocean off the coast of Cape Cod?" Suzette replied, tartly. "It's like jumping into an ice bucket, even if you're wearing a wetsuit."

The boys laughed.

"Well, this part of the Atlantic is like a bathtub . . . a big warm bathtub," Gary assured her, pulling his shirt over his head.

The girls glanced at each other.

"Ah, we're not about to undress in front of you guys like strippers," Suzette announced. "I mean, we trust you not to try anything weird, but . . ."

The thought of taking their clothes off still made the girls uncomfortable. Still, they giggled as they turned their backs and faced the sand dunes.

"You two guys go on," Suzette hollered into the wind. "We'll meet you in the water."

"Don't go out past the second waves," John shouted as he ran toward the waves.

When the girls turned around, they spotted two blurry forms disappearing into the water—brown on the top and white on the bottom. For a second, Suzette wished she was wearing her glasses. She folded her bra and panties neatly inside her shorts and placed her blouse on top of the pile. Then she ran with the others as fast as they could in the direction of the boys' voices and waded until they stood in shoulder-deep water.

"Pretty nice out here, huh?" Gary said

"Yeah, it really is," Suzette looked back towards the beach.

The conversation turned to basketball and Suzette quickly lost interest. She looked up at the sky and squinted at the constellations. Gary's arms were flailing as he described some hoop maneuver, so Suzette moved away to avoid being hit in the boob. She could hear the girls' laughter, as she flipped on her back and floated for a better view of the night sky.

It was so peaceful, here. Without streetlights or traffic noise, the beach was pure paradise.

She tried standing but discovered that her feet couldn't find the bottom. She turned toward the sound of waves breaking and swam toward shore. Finally, her feet landed on sandy bottom and she stood. But apart from the sound of water, she heard nothing. Not a single voice.

Oh, shit. They're all probably sitting up on the beach, waiting for me to walk up stark naked. No way. That's not happening.

SIX

John wiped the water from his eyes and stared down the beach.

Uh-oh. Are those lights coming toward us?"

Gary turned.

"Looks like it. Come on, guys, I left my wallet in my shorts," he said. "Let's get dressed before people find us."

"Suzette?" John heard nothing as the group ran out of the water.

"Maybe she walked back to the car," Gary said, pulling his shirt over his head.

"Um, we don't think so." The other girls stood around Suzette's folded pile of clothing a few feet from where he stood.

"Is that her stuff?" John looked surprised.

Worried, the boys raced up and down the beach, yelling Suzette's name.

Silence.

"We need some light out here," Gary said. "Let's try to get the car up on the dunes and turn on the headlights."

"We need help." They stared at each other in a state of panic.

Gary remembered a local bar with a pay phone only a few miles down the road. But when he and John reached the Camaro, they saw its wheels were stuck in the soft sand.

"Keep the wheels straight and using a very light touch on the gas pedal, rock the car forward and back by switching between drive and reverse."

Gary slid behind the wheel and turned the key in the ignition.

"Stop, the tires are spinning," John yelled into the driver's window. "Change direction."

He was concerned about Suzette getting caught in a possible rip current, a fast and narrow current running offshore. His stomach twisted painfully.

"We have to dig the sand out by hand, either in front of or behind all four tires."

The boys dug all the way to the bottom of each tire with their bare hands and added a three-foot long channel towards the street.

"Girls, grab the floor mats and flip them over so that the rubber side faces up," Gary panted.

"Take the short side of the mat and shove it under a tire."

John searched the car trunk and pulled the metal lid off a cooler, wedging it under one wheel to gain traction.

"I wish we had plywood or towels or one of my mother's stupid Persian rugs," Gary fumed. "I need to get something under these tires besides sand."

John stared at his friend.

"Speaking of your mother, you better call her when you get to a phone."

He struggled with one recurring and horrifying thought: Sharks feed at night and they tend to attack people. Every surfer knows the lack of visibility in the dark makes it easier for them to mistake humans for one of their favorite meals. He couldn't remember if Suzette was wearing any jewelry. Shiny jewelry can resemble the scales of a fish when sharks are hunting. Fortunately, he thought, she's naked. Her bright yellow bikini would attract sharks.

"If this doesn't work, we can try letting air out of the tires. You can re-inflate them when you get back on solid ground."

Suddenly the Camaro lurched backward, through the sand and onto the street. Gary stepped on the gas and the tires screeched as he drove off toward the bar.

John ran back down to the beach, shouting Suzette's name into the wind and making deals with God. *Please let her live. I am not going to tell the Captain and Mrs. LeBlanc that their daughter drowned while out with me. Swimming. In the nude.*

He was terrified.

SEVEN

Suzette squatted in waist-deep water just off shore. Her fingertips were shriveled like raisins and she was getting cold. Where were those guys? Where were her *clothes*? She was not about to walk down the beach naked. She couldn't even see very well. Something brushed against her foot and she screamed.

Well, I guess I'll just float while I wait for those losers.

She flipped on her back and looked up at the stars, squinting. If she had her glasses she could look for the short line of three stars that form Orion's belt or the large triangle of fairly bright stars that comprise Capricornus, the sea goat. She hated being legally blind because she missed seeing so much. You can't wear glasses every-where . . . like when you're swimming, for example.

Floating along with the ocean blocking her ears, Suzette was unaware that the current carried her even farther away from her friends.

John grew hoarse, his voice almost gone. He had an overwhelming sense of dread that the night would not end well. How could he ever explain the situation to his parents? To *her* parents? To the police? God, they had been stupid.

He had figured that Gary would be back soon. Hopefully with search lights and a lot more people to cover the long stretch of sand. Still, he had cupped his hands and continued to holler Suzette's name into the wind.

When her feet touched a sand bar, she stood and thought she heard something — or *someone* — shouting. A wave crashed on shore and in the moment of stillness that followed, she heard a single, unmistakable word. It was the most beautiful sound ever uttered.

"*Suzette . . .*"

"What?"

John ran into the water and splashed toward her as she bobbed in front of him.

"Oh my God," he gasped. "We thought we lost you. Come on. We've got to let Gary know you're alive."

Standing in the waist-deep water, Suzette wrapped her arms around her chest, and didn't budge.

"Do you have a *towel*?"

He stopped and shook his head. Of course — she was naked.

He peeled off his own shirt, turned away and extended an arm. It might have been the strain of the night coupled with the terror of maybe never seeing her again, or the overwhelming relief of finding her alive and modestly concerned with covering up. John started to laugh and didn't stop until his knees gave way, and he collapsed on the sand.

Suzette looked at him like he was crazy, his laughter was contagious and she started to giggle, too.

When they reached the beach, he threw his arm over her shoulders and noticed she was shivering. As they walked back towards the dunes, Suzette was amazed to see groups of people with flashlights and — *wait, is that a policeman?*

Gary's mother saw her first. The woman was as pale as a ghost as she wrapped Suzette in a blanket. "Oh, honey, we're so glad to find you."

Suzette raised her eyebrows. *Where did all these people come from?*

"All right young man, I'd like to know what went on, here," said the policeman looking grim. He switched off his searchlight and put his hands on his hips.

"Well, sir, we were skinny-dipping." John gulped for air — almost out of voice.

Suzette thought she saw the corners of the policeman's mouth twitch.

"I moved a few feet away from everyone and I guess the current swept me farther down the beach," she whispered.

People who had joined in the search began shaking hands with Gary's parents before heading to their cars. The girls, who had been crying, ran to hug Suzette. His mother stepped in and slid an arm around Suzette's blanketed waist, guiding everyone to the family station wagon.

"The boys gave me your clothes, but I think you might want a nice, hot bath when we get back to the house," she said in her soft, southern drawl. "I'm glad you're alright, sweetie. I know this would never have happened with

Gary's old girlfriend because she'd have stayed real close to those boys, naked or not. Know what I mean?" She winked. "Let's get you home."

EIGHT

Suzette expected the third degree when she got home on Sunday afternoon, but her mother said very little. "Gary's mother was sweet to call and fill me in on your adventures at the beach last night," she chuckled. "I'm glad everyone was safe."

Suzette blinked.

What, no interrogation?

"Yeah, everyone just got separated," she said, trying to sound matter of fact. "It was no big deal."

Except for the police and the search parties . . . and the sharks feeding at night, of course.

Mom took a steadying breath and watched as Suzette hoisted her overnight bag over one shoulder and headed for her bedroom. She choked back a small sob that leapt out of nowhere and Suzette turned around.

"I don't think we need to mention this to your father." Mom paused. "You know, honey, I've spent my whole life trying to protect you. I think I've done a pretty good job of it. I tried to help you as we moved from state to state, from school to school, and everywhere the Navy transferred us. But I don't know what to do with a teenager who wants her independence. How in the world can I protect you now?"

Suzette dropped her bag and hugged her mother. "Don't worry, Mom. I'll be careful and I promise I'll never go skinny-dipping again."

Monday morning arrived, along with the predictable routine of classes at Our Lady of Perpetual Guilt.

"Life is a real conundrum," Julie said, dabbing Clearasil on a red spot in the middle of her chin. "Guys say they want us to look natural, but there's nothing 'natural' about looking natural."

"Is that a quote from Max Factor or Estee Lauder?" Suzette poked her friend in the arm. "On Saturday, John and I drove to Ormond Beach and we had dinner."

"Oh my God, you went on a date with him." Julie dropped her mirror.

"It was not a date," Suzette protested. "There were loads of other people in the car."

"If you eat food with a guy, it's a date. That's just how it is. Check the handbook."

"If that's true, then I've dated half the population at our school," Suzette replied.

Julie stared off into space. "Y' know, I kind of feel sorry for all of the midshipmen at that boarding school. Those guys don't meet girls in their daily classes, don't get their phone numbers so they can memorize speeches to recite when they call. They don't really learn how to date like normal guys. It's pretty weird, I think."

Suzette agreed. "Yeah, but I don't get many phone calls from *normal* guys, either."

At least if she ever did, she could close her door and talk privately since Mom recently put an extension phone in her bedroom. The other phone hung on the kitchen wall—which allowed any conversation occurring there, to echo through the whole apartment. The curly phone cord wasn't long enough for the person talking to walk very far, so Suzette could hear every word her parents said during *their* phone calls—even when she was standing at her bathroom sink.

I have as much privacy in that place, as the inmates in prison do.

Julie pulled her peanut butter, banana, and marshmallow sandwich out of a brown paper bag and stared at it thoughtfully.

"Do you think it's a coincidence that attending our religion class feels like a penance?"

Suzette laughed and answered automatically. "Penance is defined as voluntary self-punishment inflicted as an outward expression of repentance for having done wrong. See also *atonement*."

Julie applauded. "You deserve an 'A' for memorizing vocabulary terms, girlfriend. Seriously, our teacher is definitely new to the staff at Our Lady of Perpetual Guilt, and I heard the office secretary say he dropped out of some seminary recently. I try not to look at him while he's lecturing because he's constantly pulling on his facial hair. *Ugh.* By the end of the term, I bet he won't have any beard left at all."

Suzette agreed. "Oh Lord, I *never* look at him because the hair-pulling thing drives me crazy. I *did* like discussing the play *Jesus Christ Superstar*, though. Great music and a lot better than the old Baltimore Catechism debates."

Julie nodded. "On some level, it's nice to have a religion teacher exposing us to modern ideas about Jesus, like whether he got married, had any siblings or children. Do you suppose our principal knows about the crazy curriculum he's teaching impressionable young students like us?"

"God only knows," Suzette said, grinning wickedly. "I'm not sure why the guy prints out lots of sloppy handouts with weird misspellings in Greek. The one that bothered me most was the 'kyrigma'. What the heck are we supposed to make of that? Are we supposed to be learning nonsense Greek words in a Catholic school?"

Julie leaned toward her friend and lowered her voice to a whisper. "I think several of the guys who sit in the back of the room launched a campaign to disrupt the class with dumb questions. I kind of regret my involvement in this, but I encouraged them." She covered her face with her hands. "We're going to hell. I can feel it."

Suzette wiped the last bit of lunch from her mouth. "Or, at the very least, we may be going to detention, my friend."

Detention might have been preferable to dinner that night.

Cheerleading practice took longer than usual so Suzette was late getting to the dinner table. The Captain's face was flushed and she heard ice cubes clinking as he swirled the brown liquid around in his glass.

"I had an interesting conversation with one of my midshipmen, today. A young man named Gary apologized for taking you skinny-dipping at the beach."

Suzette froze, fork wavering halfway between the plate and her mouth. She didn't notice him clenching his fists as she began, "I didn't think . . ."

"No, you didn't think," he snarled as he lurched to his feet. Enraged, he grabbed Suzette's shirt collar so hard he nearly strangled her and yanked her from the chair. He shoved her against the wall, knocking a framed portrait of Suzette and her sister sideways on its hook.

"Paul, let go of her." Mom pulled frantically on his arm. Suzette watched her mother fight back tears. "I mean it. Stop it now or I'm leaving and taking our daughter with me."

The Captain released Suzette as quickly as he had seized her. Picking up his drink from the table, he strode from the room. Suzette slid into her chair and stared at her mother. "What's *wrong* with him?"

Mom's hands shook as she straightened the portrait on the wall.

"He probably took some of his allergy medicine and it doesn't mix well with alcohol. I'm sure your father will apologize in the morning."

Suzette bit the inside of her lip. *I doubt it.*

NINE

Without her glasses or contact lenses, Suzette didn't recognize anyone who stood more than four feet away. Most of the midshipmen looked alike anyway, with their military uniforms and matching haircuts. Yet, she always could spot John because of his gait, the toe of one foot turned in slightly as he walked and his shoulders swung. He reminded her of Mr. Spock on *Star Trek*. Suzette always preferred the character Spock to Captain Kirk, anyway.

"Have you ever been to Park Avenue in Winter Park?" he asked.

Of course, she and her mother had been many times to the glitzy strip of bustling cafes with sidewalk seating, cool boutiques, and art galleries. North of Orlando, the city was nestled among a sprawling chain of lakes and dreamy, southern oaks. Many of her classmates from Our Lady of Perpetual Guilt lived nearby. The main street — Park Avenue — oozed southern charm throughout all eight blocks of its shopping and dining district. Yet

Suzette suspected that spending a day there with John would be a lot more fun than a day with Mom.

"I hear that people go to the annual Winter Park Sidewalk Art Festival," John said. "I thought you might like to go with me on Saturday and check it out."

"Really? That sounds great."

"The artists set up at nine, so why don't we leave Sanford around then? One of the guys offered to loan me his car for the day. We won't have to walk."

Suzette felt her face flush and her cheeks hurt from smiling so much. She didn't even mind when Gary walked up to them and started talking. "What are you two so happy about? Planning more skiing lessons? We can use my boat."

John shook his head, steering the conversation to an upcoming football game. Suzette was thrilled he didn't mention the art festival to Gary. *I'd rather spend the time alone with John, without his friend trailing along.*

Saturday morning, John arrived at her door out of uniform, looking spectacularly normal. Messy, curly hair, white shirt under a blue sweater, khaki pants, and brown leather ankle boots. He reached for her hand as he helped her into the car. Suzette glowed. *If this date ends right here, it will still be one of the best days of my life.* She inhaled a fragrance of shampoo and woodsy soap. He smelled amazing.

"So where should we start?" she asked. "Because I'm planning on being impressed."

They wandered down row after row of artists' booths scattered across the grand lawn that sat right in the center of the festival.

"And we get to hold hands the whole time," John said smiling. "Kinda romantic."

Suzette's heart fluttered.

She forced her eyes to focus on a group of woven baskets displayed in a booth ahead of them. Next to it, oil paintings of the water beckoned—there was so much to see!

They walked the length of the street until they reached police barricades signaling the end of the art show. Then, they turned to view the exhibitor booths lining the *opposite* side of Park Avenue.

"You're not too tired? It's getting late," John said.

"No worries. I'm tough."

They walked another block before Suzette calmed down enough to realize the butterflies in her stomach had been replaced by hunger pangs. She could smell garlic aromas coming from a nearby restaurant. He must have heard her stomach growling, because John turned to her.

"Want to get something to eat?"

They found an empty table at a sidewalk café and watched the world move around them. Suzette vaguely noticed streetlights coming on, candles twinkling on tabletops, art festival patrons hurrying past. But all she heard was John, laughing as he played with her fingers on the table. Suzette knew they were invisible to everyone but each other.

He leaned over and kissed her. Suzette was dizzy with a sort of longing that suddenly overwhelmed her. His mouth was so soft. She could get used to this.

"Second kisses are even better than the first ones," he whispered.

"I can't wait for the third."

"I know what you mean." He was grinning.

After dinner they held hands as they walked slowly back to their car.

"I'm *very* impressed with the Sidewalk Art Festival," Suzette said, finally.

John smiled and leaned against the car, pulling her close. "I hoped you would be."

Her heart raced as she wrapped her arms around his waist. "One day, maybe we'll hang *your* art in a booth here."

Later, as Suzette unlocked the front door of the apartment, she and John heard shouting inside the hallway.

"This is a naval academy and haircuts are a required part of our dress code. Do you understand, lieutenant?" The Captain's face was crimson as he bellowed at a young man standing at attention.

"Sir, yes Sir." The kid looked terrified.

At that moment, Skipper jumped at the kid's pant leg, frantic for attention. "Get down," the Captain snarled. When she didn't obey, he bent down and struck the dog hard. She whimpered. Suzette scooped up the quaking Skipper as John sprang into action.

John caught the Captain's arm as he staggered, slightly off-balance. "Let me handle this situation for you, Sir," John said quickly. "Lieutenant, I order you to meet me on the Quarterdeck."

Surprised, the Captain muttered, "Thank you, Battalion Commander" and nodded curtly before he turned to head back to his recliner. Suzette could smell the alcohol as she carried Skipper to her bedroom.

Never argue with a drunk. There's no point in trying to have a rational conversation with someone who has been drinking.

John followed the midshipman out and turned toward Suzette with a mixture of sadness and sympathy in his eyes. As he gently closed the apartment door, he silently mouthed the words, "I'm sorry."

Living with John would never be like this.

TEN

An early morning breeze blew the curtains aside from Suzette's window. She yawned and waited for her alarm clock to buzz.

"*R-O-A-R.*" Her eyes flew open.

What was that? It sounded like a lion. I know some of the guys upstairs act like animals, but this is ridiculous.

"*R-O-A-R, Grrrr.*" She sat up in bed.

"Mom, can you come in here a minute?" she shouted.

Another "*R-O-A-R*" rumbled through the window as Mom appeared in the doorway and cocked her head to listen.

"The lions are probably hungry," Mom said. "Remember, the Sanford Municipal Zoo is only a few blocks away from us. Sound travels easily in the early morning hours when it's quiet like this."

Suzette peered out of her window cautiously, to be sure no escaped lions were sitting underneath it. She remembered many of the midshipmen talking about visiting the zoo in their free time and throwing cigarettes into cages just to watch chimpanzees puff on them.

In a way I guess they're kindred spirits, although the midshipmen live in a different kind of cage.

She walked to the closet and pulled out a gray, pleated uniform skirt. By the time she was dressed and eating breakfast, Suzette could faintly hear a bugler playing *Reveille* in the halls upstairs.

"My alarm clock is bad enough, but I'm *so* glad I don't have to jump out of bed and run into the hallway every morning in my underwear," she said.

"Me, too," Mom said, stirring spoonfuls of sugar into her hot tea. "But that's the way they take attendance in a military school. Senior officers like Big Mac and John walk up and down, counting heads, to be sure that every boy who lives in their hall is up."

The Captain walked into the kitchen and poured a cup of coffee. "I want to check on the roses before Morning Formation," he announced.

Suzette carried her cereal bowl to the sink. "What, exactly, is the purpose of Morning Formation?"

The Captain cleared his throat. "We check to be sure everyone's shoes and brass belt buckles are shined to a mirror finish. The officers of each company—Halsey Company, Decatur Company, Truxton Company, and the Drill Team—do their own roll call to ensure everyone is present and accounted for. Occasionally, there have been a few runaways. Then, we raise the flag and make the day's announcements."

That's such a complicated way to take attendance.

After brushing her teeth, Suzette grabbed her books and waited by the car for Mom to drive her to catch the bus at the local Catholic church. She watched the Captain—in full uniform—spraying the rose bushes planted in front of the school for bugs. It bothered her to see how different he was during the *day*, talkative and involved with the midshipmen. She couldn't understand how his personality changed so dramatically at night, when the man retreated to a recliner with his cocktail and never spoke.

As she watched the nicer version of the Captain, she knew that soon there would be vases full of flowers in the family's apartment and possibly on the desk of the school secretary, too. Just then, Big Mac walked down the front steps and waved at her.

"Good morning, everyone. Sir, your roses are looking pretty good."

"The groundskeeper told me they bloom year-round in the central parts of the state," the Captain said. "Roses need direct sunlight for at least six hours a day. Morning sunlight is best because it dries the dew to stop fungus from growing. Did you notice that more flowers are produced during summer than in the cooler seasons?" he asked.

Big Mac shook his head and Suzette squinted more closely at the blooms.

"Personally, I think the flowers seem larger and have more petals during the cooler months," the Captain continued. "Rose growers recommend they should be fertilized once a month from February to November."

The Captain removed the faded flowers. "They call it dead-heading," he said with a wink. "It's a little like the school barbershop. I'm selectively trimming the plants to keep them healthy, well-shaped, and productive. It also directs all the plant energy into new growth and blooms."

As he spoke, he removed dead twigs and canes that looked injured or spindly.

"It regulates the height, improves the air circulation, and light penetration within the plant," he explained.

"We'll see the first flowers eight to nine weeks after I finish pruning."

Suzette was puzzled. "Why doesn't the groundskeeper do it?"

"Takes too much time," the Captain responded, brushing dirt from his hands. "He rakes the area under the bush to remove all the dead and diseased leaves. Then he has to mulch immediately to create a barrier between the plant and the spores on the ground. That stops fungus from splashing onto the plant and re-infecting it. I start spraying as soon as new growth emerges and continue throughout the growing season."

"Seems like an awful lot of work." Suzette shook her head.

"Most things in life are," the Captain answered as he headed toward his office. "Every great success requires some type of struggle to get there. Good things take time."

Big Mac chuckled as he told Suzette about solving his first crisis of the day.

"This little kid who lives on my hall was so upset because he didn't grab the toilet paper and bring it into his room fast enough. He didn't know what to do."

Huh?

Seeing Suzette's puzzled expression, Big Mac explained. "Once a week, the custodian leaves rolls of toilet paper outside each midshipman's door. Unfortunately, the rolls often are stolen by older guys, who stockpile them in their room. It's the cheapest, thinnest toilet paper so people are afraid of running out. The school needs to order better stuff."

"Mike McGrath, please report to the commandant's office immediately."

They both heard the voice blaring over a loudspeaker and Big Mac gathered his books. "Have a good day. I don't know why your dad needs me, but I might see you and your mom later."

Big Mac ambled into the Captain's office. "You wanted to speak to me, sir?"

He noticed the hard set of the Captain's jaw, an expression usually reserved for disciplinary actions.

"Yes, Mac, please have a seat."

The Captain pulled a sheet of paper out of his desk drawer.

"I received an anonymous letter stating that you are selling drugs to midshipmen out of your room. I want to give you a chance to explain."

Big Mac burst out laughing.

"Seriously, sir? It must be a joke."

The Captain immediately looked relieved. He linked his hands behind his head, working the facts over again.

"Son, I'm taking this threat seriously. Your room isn't secure, and *anyone* could plant drugs in there to get you into a ton of trouble. I want you to know that I'm notifying the FBI as well as our school superintendent. I want to protect you from any fallout if the author of this letter decides to take things a step further."

"Thank you, sir," Big Mac said, slowly. "I have absolutely no idea who might want to cause trouble for me."

He walked back outside the building where Suzette stood waiting for her mother. Another midshipman named Gary stood with her, and Suzette didn't look too happy about it.

Big Mac ignored the other boy. "The weirdest thing just happened," he said, repeating the conversation with the Captain.

"Didn't you once tell me about some of the guys on the football team, who wanted — no, *demanded* — that you try out for the team?" Suzette lowered her voice. "When you said no, could they be mad enough to try to get you expelled? Or maybe even arrested? How far would they go?"

"I'll ask around and let you know if I hear anything." Gary tried to sound helpful, though he looked worried.

Big Mac shrugged. "I don't know. I guess it doesn't really matter who wrote the letter because the Captain has my back."

ELEVEN

Suzette put a hand on her hip and blocked John's path.

"So, are you ignoring me or just playing hard to get?"

John shrugged and ran his hand through his hair in a way that was adorable. "Well, you *are* kind of intimidating."

"What do you mean?" She felt the color creep into her cheeks

"The way you walk through the quarterdeck, sort of dismissing everyone."

"Are you asking me or telling me that's what I do?" Suzette was angry. "Don't make fun of me, John. You know, I can't *see* anyone if I'm not wearing my glasses."

She shook her head and screwed her eyes shut in embarrassment. When she opened them, he was staring at her. Immediately, he took her elbow and steered her around the corner to a quiet spot beside the stairwell.

Then he kissed her, and her brain went into meltdown mode. When they pulled apart, she wasn't sure whether they had been together for a minute, an hour, or a year.

"I'm sorry I sounded like such a jerk," he murmured into her hair. "And I'm sorry that I sometimes forget that your big blue eyes give you problems."

They walked back to the quarterdeck together, straight into Gary.

"What are you two kids up to?" He leered at them in a way that made Suzette uncomfortable.

Luckily, at that moment Big Mac and five other boys, out of uniform and wearing golfing attire, headed out of the school's front doors. The team stopped abruptly at the foot of the stairs.

"What in the hell . . ." Big Mac stared.

Suzette and John followed them to see a battleship-gray hearse parked in front of the school. Bigger than a station wagon, the large vehicle was originally used to carry coffins from a church or funeral home to a cemetery.

Big Mac's golf bag dropped from his shoulder to the ground. "Um, exactly *where* are we playing this match?"

The golf coach slid from the driver's seat. "Isn't this great, guys? The golf team was too small for a bus, but this hearse is the perfect size for us. I think the school bought it from a surplus sale at the old Orlando Navy base."

The coach swung open a large door at the back of the vehicle. The flat space inside included a few rollers in the bed, designed to slide caskets in and out.

Suzette covered her mouth with her hand to keep from laughing, but one midshipman could barely contain his excitement. "It's wicked! Coach, I've seen old pictures of hearses that had a metal framework with a lot of spikes to hold burning candles. This one must be newer, though."

"Stop reading *Dracula*," someone else muttered.

"Think how easy it will be to get our clubs out," the coach enthused. "Just don't sit on the rollers, boys, or you might feel it if we hit a bump in the road. And this thing's got a big V-8 engine under the hood, so we'll get to our matches in no time."

"I call shotgun," Big Mac announced. "I'm taller than the rest of you, so I get the front seat."

Suzette watched five midshipmen scramble into the hearse, their golf bags wedged between them.

"No seat belts back there, huh?" Suzette turned to John, who shrugged.

"Normally, I guess no one needs 'em in that vehicle," he said. "I'm sure the guys will be fine."

"Hey, there's no door handle back here," one team member shouted out the window.

"I guess it was designed for occupants who didn't try to get *out* of it," Suzette said, laughing. "Dead people don't need door handles."

Neither Suzette nor the golf team could have imagined the effect their arrival would have on the other high school teams participating in the tournament. Jaws dropped as the coach parked the hearse at the golf course. Big Mac walked around and opened the back door of the hearse with flourish. One by one, the five team mates scrambled from the rear compartment and slung golf bags over their shoulders.

Big Mac turned to a player from another team who gaped as he clutched a scorecard and pencil.

"What's were you expecting . . . a coffin?"

TWELVE

Suzette loved living a short drive from the beach. On Saturdays, John would borrow a car from one of the midshipmen who kept them illegally stashed nearby. In order to reduce its liability, the naval academy didn't allow students to have cars. It was clearly stated in the rules for admission and most families were delighted to comply. But a handful of resourceful midshipmen found parking garages—or local girls on the cheerleading squad who would keep their cars parked discreetly during the week.

Walking along the water's edge, watching sandpipers run in and out with the tide, and just breathing the salt air removed all the tensions and anxieties leftover from the week. It felt magical.

They listened to the Beach Boys on the radio until John reached over and squeezed Suzette's hand.

"I see, sometimes, how your dad upsets you," he started.

Embarrassed, she started to protest but he continued.

"My own father is a big fan of the three-martini lunch, much to my mother's dismay. The businessman's disease is what she calls it. Growing up, I learned pretty quickly that when someone is out of control, it makes sense to avoid contact with them, if you can. I watched my older brothers, who showed me that you can't argue with someone who is drinking. Whenever I'm home for a visit, I just leave the room when I see that my father's had too much. Why do you think I chose to go to a boarding school like the naval academy? I had to remove myself from the situation because my life got so miserable."

Suzette's eyes widened.

"Before I got out of the house, it helped me to talk with someone I trusted. Sometimes it was a friend or my brother, but other times it was a guidance counselor or a coach."

He gave her a rueful grin.

"The strange thing is, even though I don't live at home any more, my father's drinking still affects me. It sounds weird, but I get uneasy when my life is going smoothly. It's like I always anticipate problems."

Listening to John talk about his family and the way he dealt with the alcoholic in *his* life, gave her a strange sense of relief. They had the same story, just slightly different details. If they had a home together, she knew it would never be like the ones they grew up in.

"I totally get it," she said. "Alcoholism is a family disease. It's frustrating for those of us who *live* with it not to be able to *control* it. It's just so hard to escape from all the tension in my house. I can't wait to go to college."

At the stop light, they kissed until the car behind them started honking and then it took a few seconds for them to untangle themselves from one another. A late afternoon sunset was taking a bow.

"You are the best thing that ever happened to me," John said.

Suzette felt like her heart was beating too hard, aching with every kind word.

She pretended to punch him in the stomach and he jumped back in the seat. "Yikes, that violent streak of yours kind of turns me on."

She inspected herself in the rear-view mirror and touched her hair, which looked disheveled. It was funny. With John she never worried about how she looked. All that mattered was how she *felt*.

"I wish we could start our lives together right now," she whispered. "It's going to be weird here, without you next year."

He sighed. "It's scary, you know? Moving. Leaving the academy, where I've lived for the past four years. Not leaving my *parents*, of course."

Suzette appreciated all the noisy conversation at the table every time Big Mac and John stayed for dinner. They rarely ate on the Mess Deck with other midshipmen any more, preferring Mom's cooking (and more likely, her company) to the soggy vegetables that were standard cafeteria fare. Occasionally, Gary wrangled an invitation from Mom, too.

All of the boys laughed over a new student's confusion with naval terminology.

"The teacher said, '*Keep the head clean, gentlemen*,' and this little kid's eyes flew open," Big Mac chortled. "I swear he asked whose head he needed to clean. He had no idea that a *head* is a *bathroom*."

"Don't you remember how weird everything sounded in the beginning?" John said, giggling. "I had no idea *liberty* meant freedom for a sailor to go ashore, or go downtown, in our case."

"True," Big Mac said. "When one of the older guys mentioned *Passing Muster*, I thought he said *mustard*."

John howled with laughter.

"Well, what *does* it mean?" Suzette asked.

"To gather soldiers in a group to show officers they are acceptably dressed and equipped," they answered in unison.

"After four years here, I guess we all understand nautical vocabulary," Big Mac acknowledged. "It's kind of like learning Spanish or French, I guess. It's a new language. Thank you very much for dinner, Mrs. LeBlanc."

He turned to John. "I've got an exam to study for, so I guess I'll see you back upstairs in the room."

Mom walked with him out to the school corridor and Gary reluctantly followed as the Captain headed to his recliner. Suzette heard the *clink* of ice cubes in a glass, which filled her with dread. She avoided having friends over for her entire life because she didn't want anyone to know that her dad drank too much. It wasn't until her freshman year of high school that she felt the full weight of it. These midshipmen were older, and they could tell the difference between a sober Captain and a hammered one.

She looked at John and motioned toward the front door.

Sitting on the front step of the apartment, she curled up against John's arm, wrapping her hand around his. Their hands stayed together until the last possible moment, until just their fingertips touched.

"I should go. The troops are waiting upstairs."

Suzette groaned and dropped her head against his shoulder. She felt his arm around her, like a hug, like a home.

She walked John out to the corridor as slowly as possible, trying to spend as much time with him as she could before he had to go back to the cell upstairs that constituted his bedroom.

"See you tomorrow," he smiled.

Later, she dreamed she was chasing John down the beach, the curls in his hair getting smaller and smaller until she couldn't see them anymore.

THIRTEEN

Suzette was always grateful when her mother didn't ask how John managed to borrow a car to drive to the beach. She figured her mother wasn't worried about her having sex, since there isn't much privacy at a public beach. She and John would park the car, spread out a blanket and eat sandwiches they bought at a cozy French bakery they passed on the way. They threw seashells into the water between the waves and listened for the splash.

"I hope some day we can live by the water," Suzette said wistfully. "I love it, here."

John grabbed her hand and kissed the back of it. "Yeah, me too. Sitting out on the dock at my parents' house relaxes me, no matter what's going on inside. I promise we'll work on getting a house by the water one day."

Watching pelicans was their favorite pastime. The birds waddled awkwardly on land, yet looked so graceful when they circled overhead. Riding the air currents, they would suddenly plummet out of the sky, one by one, diving straight into the water with a loud splash. Seconds later they would surface with a fish in their beak.

"A marvelous bird is the pelican," Suzette recited. "His mouth can hold more than his belly can."

"I see you study the classics," John said.

"Ogden Nash was the best poet, ever." She smiled and passed the potato chip bag. "Save me the burnt ones, please."

John merely nodded and waited while Suzette sipped her Dr. Pepper.

They lingered, watching the waves throw themselves onto the beach, until dark blue clouds started to form, heavy with the threat of rain. Suzette felt a burst of cool air from the approaching storm and hurried to shake the sand from the blanket. John loaded their cooler in the trunk. The drive home always included a stop at Dairy Whip for ice cream — the perfect ending to the perfect day.

"I used to wonder why my ice cream or jelly sandwich always tasted crunchy at the beach," Suzette admitted as they peered through the glass at the ice cream counter.

John laughed. "You never considered the blowing sand might have something to do with it? You really *are* a natural blonde, aren't you?"

A few blocks from the shop, a sudden squall caught up with them. Even with the windshield wipers at high speed they couldn't see the road, so John pulled over.

"When thunder roars, go indoors," Suzette shouted over the din. "Not quite Ogden Nash, but still important poetry. I read somewhere that a sturdy building is the safest place to be during a thunderstorm in Florida. We're supposed to avoid flooded roadways because six inches of fast-moving water can knock you down, and a foot of moving water can sweep your vehicle away."

For a moment, they just looked at each other. The blinding rain formed a protective curtain around them. She was in a car with someone she hadn't known very long, and yet it felt like the most natural thing in the world to lean forward, as John did, until they were face-to-face.

Lightning illuminated the sky and they jumped apart. Silence. Except from her heart, which was pounding in her chest and ears so loudly she was sure John could hear it, too.

It's amazing to feel so connected to a guy. The day wasn't even close to over, but she could think of nothing more than how she didn't want it to end.

"C'mere," he said tugging her hand.

John gently put his hands on her waist and pulled her toward him. His mouth found her neck and then her ear. He was breathing hard and kissing hard. His hand moved from her thigh to her breast, through her shirt and bikini top. He groaned and whispered into her ear, "The things you do to me, Suzette."

And won't do, she reminded herself.

John had this thing where he raised one eyebrow and grinned slowly at her. It drove her totally crazy. She didn't plan on being a virgin forever, but unlike, say, making your First Communion or Confirmation, Suzette didn't think she needed to set a definite date. However, having sex with a high-school boyfriend who would leave for college in *another state* really seemed like a bad idea. She thought of the naval academy cheerleaders who had bounced in and out of many midshipmen's beds and were dumped at graduation when the boys left for college.

Real smart idea. You're a genius. Apply for a Fulbright scholarship as soon as you get a chance.

She curled up against John, her knees tucked into her chest and her head against his shoulder. She felt him smile against her hair as he wrapped his arm around her and they waited for the rain to pass.

Suzette left the gym from cheerleading practice and noticed a midshipman pacing the sidewalk in front of the school.

"Hey, Suzette, your dad really saved my neck today," he said, looking down. "A guy who graduated last year, discovered that having a military haircut and uniform has some benefits. Bouncers who guard the doors of bars and clubs let servicemen in without checking their IDs too closely. Clerks at the convenience store are the same way. I got a fake license for twenty bucks and it works."

His smile faded as he continued. "Anyway, I drove to the 7-11 and bought two six-packs. At the checkout counter, I showed the clerk my license, paid in cash and headed back to my friends waiting in the car. That's when a guy who had been behind me in line knocked on the window. Turns out he was an off-duty policeman and held up his badge. Told me he was going to arrest me for contributing to the delinquency of a minor. Worse than that, he confiscated the beer."

By then, other midshipmen had gathered around them, listening to the story.

"Did the policeman take you in jail?" Suzette asked.

"No, he drove us back to school and marched us into your dad's office. The Captain asked for my license, so I gave him my *real* one, instead of the fake. Somehow, he talked the cop out of arresting me. Could you please thank him again, for me?"

"I . . . well, sure."

She shook her head as she walked back to the apartment. *Kind of ironic that an adult with an alcohol problem protects a kid with an alcohol problem. Guess it takes one to know one.*

FOURTEEN

I 'm sorry, but the Captain isn't available. He isn't feeling well."

Mom was speaking to some kid standing outside the apartment door. Suzette looked at the clock on her nightstand. Eight o'clock. By now, the Captain definitely was feeling no pain.

Suzette's bedroom was next to the front door, which usually forced her into the role of doorman. But tonight, she was cramming for a test, so Mom stepped in. She looked up from the geometry book in time to see her mother lean against the door and sigh.

"What's going on?" Suzette asked, knowing the answer.

"Oh, nothing much." Her mother walked in and sat on the end of the other twin bed, clutching a tea cup.

Suzette took off her glasses and spoke. "C'mon, Mom. Dad denies he has a problem. He claims he doesn't need help. He probably promises you that he won't drink again. But it's not working, is it? By accepting his promises, Mom, you're denying the problem too."

Tears rolled down Mom's face, one long drip after another. She wiped her eyes with the back of her hand.

"You're too young to understand," she said. "Your father is no different from other retired military pilots. They worked hard and they played hard. They sacrificed a lot for their country."

"Does that mean they get to sacrifice their *families*, too?"

Suzette felt her own eyes begin to water, so she dug her nails into her palm. "Mom, I think I understand things pretty well. You and I deny dad's problem when we hide it from the midshipmen and pretend it doesn't exist. You deny the problem if you threaten to leave him and don't follow through. Did you ever think that Dad might be 'listening' to what you *do* and not to what you *say*?"

Suzette was used to her mother being strong and confident. She depended on it. So, when the woman surprised her with sobs it rattled Suzette to the core. Suzette was shocked to see her struggling to keep from falling apart.

"Alcoholism is a disease," Mom said slowly. "Your father uses liquor to escape from reality and responsibility. I know he feels guilty, but he can't make himself stop drinking. He is *physically* addicted to alcohol and probably would have withdrawal symptoms if he tried to stop. I'm pretty sure he's also *emotionally* dependent on booze and truly believes he can't live without it."

Suzette waited a few minutes before asking, "What can we do?"

Mom blew her nose.

"Nothing. The desire to stop drinking has to come from inside your father. No one can force an alcoholic to stop drinking. I know because I've tried for years."

Suzette rested her forehead on the heels of her hands. *Like that's ever going to happen. John would never do this to me.*

"I don't understand," she muttered. "Why aren't you angry with him?"

"Honey, sometimes I do get angry. Anger is a normal reaction to frustration and failure. I just put it to good use to change what I can. I didn't cause his drinking problem and you know what? I've discovered that I can't cure it, either."

She stroked Suzette's hair and cleared her throat. "I know it's frustrating, Sweetie, but please don't spend a lot of time worrying about your dad. All the worrying in the world won't change a thing."

FIFTEEN

W e're going to watch a rocket launch," Mom announced. "How many times can you see history being made?"

Suzette looked up from her book and raised an eyebrow. "No kidding."

"One of your dad's old navy buddies got us VIP tickets to watch the launch. It should be exciting. Your father invited Big Mac to join us."

Mom sighed deeply, a sign she was through asking and now *telling* her daughter what to do.

Suzette wasn't thrilled with the idea of a long drive to the east coast. Still, she was curious about Cape Kennedy, which stood on a sliver of land next to Merritt Island. Parts of the military base next to it had been designated a National Historic Landmark because of their connection to the early years of the American space program. Plus, if they were on the road, she figured the Captain wouldn't drink.

"We'll be watching the launch of the first spacecraft to cross the *asteroid belt*, the first to leave our Solar

System, and the first to do a fly-by of Jupiter," the Captain announced.

"Jupiter is the biggest planet," Mac said absently. Then, seeing Suzette's puzzled expression he added, "What? I liked taking science classes."

She'd watched a couple of rocket launches on television, but Suzette wasn't much of a "*space nut*".

"I remember a launch attempt in 1965 when the Atlas's fuel valves accidentally closed one second after liftoff," the Captain said. "The rocket fell back onto the launch pad and caused the biggest explosion ever seen at the Cape."

"Um, so *why* are we driving to see one up close and personal?" Suzette inquired. "I don't want to die in a fireball."

The Captain laughed. "They've fixed the problem and made a lot of improvements in the last seven years. There's nothing to worry about."

"Sir, why do they launch rockets here, in Florida?" Big Mac asked.

"Excellent question." The Captain nodded. "Cape Canaveral was chosen for launches to take advantage of the Earth's rotation. The velocity of the Earth's surface is greatest at the equator. The location of The Cape allows rockets to take advantage of this by launching eastward, in the same direction as the Earth's rotation. It's an advantage for equatorial orbits but not for highly inclined orbits such as polar orbits. It's also better to have the area sparsely populated, in case of accidents. An ocean is ideal for this. The east coast of Florida has many logistical advantages over other sites in the United States."

Suzette was confused. "Wait, where are we going? Cape Kennedy or Cape Canaveral?"

"They are one-in-the-same place," Mom explained.

"President Johnson renamed the area 'Cape Kennedy' after President John F. Kennedy, who had set the goal of landing on the moon. When Kennedy was assassinated, his widow, Jaqueline Kennedy, suggested that renaming the Cape Canaveral facility would be a nice memorial."

"I knew that," Big Mac grinned.

"Suzette, you probably don't remember because you were too little, but we watched President Johnson recommend renaming the cape in a televised address after the assassination," Mom continued. "It was so sad. Kennedy's last visit to the space facility was only six days before he died."

They pulled up to a security gate, where the Captain produced four tickets and a parking pass. *When he's sober, he's not such a bad guy. Sometimes he's actually fun to be around.*

But Suzette had learned years ago not to get her hopes up. The good times wouldn't last. She walked with Big Mac and her parents to a large, grassy area with metal bleachers that was a few miles from the launch pads.

"This is the VIP viewing area?" Suzette whispered to Big Mac. He grinned and shrugged. Mom produced a bottle of sunscreen, which they applied to their arms, legs and faces. At least there was a concession stand with snacks and refreshments available. The Captain headed for it and returned with two cans of cola for Suzette and Big Mac, along with two cans of beer. He popped the tab on Mom's before opening his own.

As she sipped, Suzette noticed there were outdoor portable toilets. She hated using those things, since the odor inside was usually awful. *Better not drink too much liquid or I'll have to pee.*

As the day dragged on, it was clear that the Captain didn't share her concern. He asked if anyone wanted anything, before returning to the concession for more beer. The metal bleachers grew hot in the sun and Suzette couldn't seem to get comfortable. As she shifted her weight for the hundredth time, the elderly couple sitting in front of her turned and smiled.

"Ever been to one of these before?" the man asked.

Suzette shook her head.

"There's something about witnessing a live rocket launch that leaves a person in awe," he said. "When the countdown ends, you'll see a big flash of fire. That's when the rocket engines ignite. You can feel the ground vibrate here, and I guarantee you'll never see anything like it again."

Time dragged on and the sun started to set. The Captain opened his fifth can of beer and Suzette had just torn open a bag of pretzels when a voice boomed from the loudspeaker.

"Ladies and gentlemen, and distinguished guests, we regret tonight's launch is cancelled for safety reasons. The soonest next launch could be tomorrow in what is known as a 'twenty-four-hour recycle.'"

The crowd groaned and some even booed as they headed for their cars.

"Even the most minor problem can lead to a cancellation," the Captain said. "After all, NASA would rather delay a launch by a day or two than waste hundreds of millions of dollars' worth of equipment."

He tripped over something in the grass but caught himself on the hood of the car before he fell.

"Dear, why don't you let me drive home?" Mom asked. "It's been a long day in the sun and I know you're tired. It sounds strange, I know, but I feel wide awake. Why don't you just rest?"

Suzette waited for an argument, but it never came. After a slight hesitation, the Captain agreed and slid into the passenger seat.

Suzette glanced at Big Mac, but he didn't seem to notice her father's sloppy state. She exhaled in relief as she buckled her seatbelt.

"I guess we'll have to see history made another time."

SIXTEEN

A week before classes ended for Christmas break, Mom swanned into Suzette's bedroom. "Since Big Mac's birthday is December tenth, and yours later in the month, your father and I thought we'd celebrate *both* of you at a luau at the Polynesian Village Hotel at Walt Disney World. Would you like to invite John to come, too?"

Do you even have to ask?

Later that night when both boys arrived at the apartment, Mom gave them an air-kiss on each cheek. They looked quite imposing in their dress blues uniforms with their officers' hats tucked under one arm. "Wow, you look like the real deal," Suzette exclaimed. "It's like you just got off an aircraft carrier or something."

Big Mac chuckled as he shook the Captain's hand. "Just as long as they don't ask for our I.D.s"

Suzette wore a flowered dress and heels to get in the island spirit. Mom insisted on embarrassing everyone by taking a picture "of the birthday boy and girl" before they left.

Walt Disney World was a half-hour drive away, which allowed plenty of time for everyone to talk about the recent Christmas Party for orphans from the Methodist Children's Home in the car. Suzette wedged herself comfortably between John and Big Mac in the back seat.

"You did a wonderful job as Santa Claus, Mac," Mom said earnestly. "It's such a nice event for the Key Club to host and a wonderful treat for the orphans. I heard lots of gasps from the children when you walked down the main staircase carrying that big sack of toys over your shoulder. I even heard jingle bells! Why did you say no when they first asked you to play Santa?"

"I was afraid of some kid pulling my beard off," Big Mac admitted. "That would have ruined the day for the rest of them. So, I came up with a plan. When they sat in my lap, I put my arm around their back and held onto their left arm. Their right arm was up against my body, so it couldn't move. And I'm happy to report that none of them tried to pull on the beard."

"You're a genius," Suzette complimented him. "What did the kids say to you?"

"Most just wanted a truck or a toy, but one boy asked me for a mommy and a daddy. A sweet little girl with blonde curls said all she wanted was someone to adopt her. That nearly killed me to hear."

Suzette blinked away tears. "How in the world did you answer them?"

"I didn't promise anything," he said, clearing his throat. "I just said you have to be a good boy or girl and I'll check my list when I get back to the North Pole."

He paused and the car was silent. John reached behind Suzette and patted Big Mac on the shoulder.

"Oh, and thanks again, Mrs. LeBlanc, for putting Noxzema cream on my eyebrows so they'd match the

white beard. I wouldn't have thought of that," he smiled.
"The guy who delivered the Santa suit gave me a few tips,
too. He told me to let the little ones stand first if they
seemed too scared to approach me. If I spoke to them
softly, they got comfortable enough sit on my lap for a
picture. It's really tough to be a convincing Santa."

"Jeez, Santa Claus is the most well-known character in
the world," Suzette said. "I bet guys like Robert Redford
and Burt Reynolds envy you."

Big Mac threw back his head and chortled.

"We're all proud of you," the Captain glanced in the
rearview mirror. "Community service is very important."

Her hand holding John's, Suzette looked at Big Mac,
sitting beside her. *This must be what it's like to have a
brother.* Their relationship was easy — despite the fact
that Big Mac loved to tease and there was never any
drama between them. Though they were born to different parents, he effortlessly shared hers.

Seated in the dining room, John pressed his knee
against Suzette's under the table. She smiled and shot
him a sidelong glance as she studied menu items like
sweet-and-sour pork, Polynesian ribs, Hawaiian chicken
and coconut bread. Mom ordered a tropical cocktail and
gave Suzette the cherry resting on top. It was attached
to a paper umbrella, which she promptly stuck behind
her ear like a hair clip. Soon, the lights dimmed and a
voice boomed "*Aloha!*" Before them shimmying dancers,
drummers, and a show-stopping fire-knife performer
gave a dazzling performance. Suzette loved the costumes
from Polynesia, along with the dances from Tahiti,
Samoa, Tonga, New Zealand, and Hawaii.

"Who knew that you could make great clothes out of
coconuts and some banana leaves?" she whispered to Big
Mac and he shook with silent laughter.

When a birthday cake arrived at the table, they both closed their eyes, made their wishes and blew out the candles. Her parents clapped with John. Mercifully, the Polynesian waiters didn't burst into song. Suzette hated listening to restaurant birthday serenades with a smile frozen on her face. It was so *embarrassing*.

Like the fall semester, the meal ended too quickly. Within days, John, Big Mac, and the other midshipmen abandoned the school and headed to their family homes throughout the country. No one — not even the losers who stayed for summer school — spent their Christmas holidays in Sanford.

"Are you going to miss me?" Gary called to her as he carried a duffle bag to his parents' car.

"I'm going to miss *everybody*," Suzette gritted her teeth and gripped Skipper's leash. "Merry Christmas!"

God, he's annoying. Always flirting or fishing for a compliment. I wish he'd just give up.

Suzette walked her dog through the eerily silent and empty Quarterdeck. She already felt lonely. At least her sister would be home from college for a few weeks. That meant someone else in the house to keep the Captain's drinking in check. Along with Mom, the sisters often sat around a twenty-foot Christmas tree that glowed in the middle of the deserted school lobby.

The tree lights look so pretty from the street — a lot of things do, when you're on the outside looking in.

Apart from the rent-a-cop making his rounds, there would be no other sign of life until January when the midshipmen returned.

The first year she lived at the naval academy, Suzette was devastated when the young men who had become such a part of her family, seemed to abandon her to return home to their biological roots. She heard every creak in the old building during the silence that lasted for weeks.

This year didn't look to be quite as depressing as the last one. Suzette figured she was more prepared for the emptiness, but she also had something to look forward to . . . she was getting her driver's license. She studied the Rules of the Road and signage in the manual until she couldn't see straight. She planned to arrive at the Florida Department of Motor Vehicles office when it opened at nine on her birthday. On the actual morning she was so nervous she could barely eat breakfast.

"I'm a little scared of the road test." She bit her lower lip. "My driver's ed teacher said the three-point turn is a critical part of the test because it's dangerous and can have serious consequences if you don't do it right." A lot of the midshipmen failed their road tests because they screwed up the three-point turn.

"I'm sure you'll do fine." Mom said. "The place shouldn't be very crowded two days after Christmas."

Suzette carried her birth certificate and proof of the driver's education course to the counter. She decided to wear her contact lenses instead of glasses and she aced the eye exam. Mom sat on the opposite side of the waiting room and read magazines while Suzette completed the written part of the exam. When she turned it in, a tall, bald man stepped from behind the counter and introduced himself as the driving examiner who would administer her road test. He looked like one of the Muppets.

They drove for a few blocks and she silently obeyed every time he issued a command. "*Turn right*" or "*Turn left*." He directed her down a quiet side street and announced, "*We will be doing a three-point turn. Please pull over to the curb and stop*."

Suzette started sweating.

She turned on the right signal light and applied the brake to let others know that she was about to stop. Checking for traffic, she turned on the left signal light and drove across the road, slowly came to a stop without crashing onto the curb. With her foot on the brake, she shifted her body to the right and glanced out the window past the examiner. Grabbing the back of the seat behind him with her right hand, Suzette pointed her head at the rear window to see when it was safe to begin moving backwards.

The drivers' ed teacher's voice echoed through her head, "*Check for traffic in your mirrors.*"

She put the car in reverse and allowed it to creep backwards.

Slow with the car, fast with the hands.

Immediately after she stopped and pressed the brake pedal firmly down, Suzette turned her head and the trunk of her body to the front. She shifted into drive, put her hands in the proper steering position, then looked to the left and right for traffic. When it was clear, she gently pushed the gas pedal and accelerated. Her breathing returned to normal.

The order to parallel park came soon after.

She pulled alongside the car ahead of the space the examiner selected. Backing up until the wad of gum she stuck in the center of the trunk lid aligned with the edge of the sidewalk, she straightened the steering wheel and continued to reverse. When the hood of her car reached the rear bumper of the one in front, she turned the wheel the other way. Miraculously, she was in the space. She wanted to get out and admire her work. Instead, she heard the examiner ask, "Are you finished?"

"Um, well yeah."

He directed her to drive back to the office, jotting notes on his clipboard as she parked the car. The silence was deafening. Mom looked up when Suzette followed the examiner through the waiting room and raised an eyebrow. Suzette shrugged.

Finally, as he faced her across the counter, the examiner spoke.

"All right, young lady. Let's get you a driver's license."

Later, as she twirled Skipper around the living room, Suzette announced, "This is the best birthday ever." Even the picture on her license turned out looking pretty good.

When the doorbell rang, she was surprised to see a floral delivery man holding a large horseshoe made of yellow roses that looked like it should be around the neck of a Kentucky Derby winner. A ribbon printed with the words, "*Good Luck*," was woven between the roses. She put her hand over her mouth and was pretty sure if her eyes got any wider, they would fall out of their sockets. The roses looked gorgeous and smelled even better. A small card tucked inside the arrangement was signed,

Good luck on your driver's test!
Big Mac + John

She didn't feel quite so forgotten, after all.

SEVENTEEN

Midshipmen arrived back on the school campus in the middle of January bragging about their holidays. Suzette was happy to hear the thuds and muffled laughter emanating from the dorm rooms above her. But she was even happier to hear John's invitation a month later.

"I want you to come home with me for the weekend. My parents have been nagging me to visit and I don't want to go without you."

"Wow I'd love to, but we better check with my mom and see if it's okay."

Suzette loved her mother, but if the woman had her way, she would wrap Suzette in cotton balls to keep her safe. Despite the fact that she adored many of the midshipmen like her own children, when it came to Suzette's personal freedom or curfews, Mom was a total dictator.

She didn't object to this trip, however. Suzette guessed it was because John's father was on the board of trustees for the naval academy that Mom seemed unconcerned.

"Why don't you bring this with you?" Mom held a pale lavender dress with a high neck and short sleeves she had plucked from the closet. "It's not too short and I think it would be very appropriate to wear if they take you out to dinner."

Suzette nodded, knowing that John's parents were old enough to be her grandparents. She enjoyed spending time with the families of her friends from Our Lady of Perpetual Guilt and she wanted to get to know John's family better since someday, they would be *her* family, too.

Though she guessed that John's parents had money, she wasn't fully prepared for *how much*. All around their home were signs of the good life — Oriental rugs (priceless, she guessed), silver-framed photographs, an ornately framed painting of someone's ancestor. At that moment Suzette was glad her grandmother had taught her a bit about antiques. She recognized an eighteenth-century Venetian chandelier softly illuminating the room. The home boasted a look of prosperity that came with professional success, and an appreciation of tradition.

Suzette also understood when Mom suggested she pack some conservative clothing. Years of moving and changing schools had shown her that women really dressed for other women. Guys didn't notice clothes, in her experience, or if they did, they only noticed what you left *uncovered*. How could she possibly pull on a halter top in front of John's mother, who dressed like the Queen of England? (Minus the tiara, of course.)

F. Scott Fitzgerald's quote drifted back to her: "The rich are very different from you and me," along with Ernest Hemmingway's response, "Yes, they have more money."

John's mother escorted her to a pristine guest room, where twin beds were adorned with monogrammed coverlets. Piles of pillows in crisp antique linens screamed "don't touch." It was like stepping into a pastel dream. Even the white towels were monogrammed! Suzette was terrified of soiling them with mascara or makeup.

Dinner reservations at The Club called for a change from the shorts Suzette wore when she arrived. A distinctly private place, the John's Island Club appeared to exist for the exclusive purpose of providing first class services for its members and their guests.

She slipped into the slightly wrinkled dress she had packed in her bag and ballet flats. Perched on the foot of the bed, she bent over and put her hands on her knees, taking a few deep breaths to calm the butterflies in her stomach. She straightened and walked to the living room, where John and his father sat gazing at a stunning view of the water through a large picture window. They stood when she entered — like good Southern gentlemen — and offered her something to drink. John sipped ginger ale while his father's glass held something resembling the Captain's nightly highballs. The three chatted politely until John's mother appeared in a silk sheath, pearls, and high heels.

As the women picked up their purses to leave, John's father broke into an impromptu tap dance in the foyer and Suzette giggled. It seemed so out of character for the stoic man in the suit and tie, she thought it hilarious until she glanced at John's mother. The woman's face twisted into an expression of annoyance and disapproval that Suzette had witnessed often enough on her own mother. Wordlessly it said, "*My husband has had too much to drink, again.*"

John's father flung his arms wide open as he pirouetted in a circle. A crystal vase crashed to the floor from the console table, scattering long-stemmed roses and water across the marble. His wife's face morphed to horror and then, utter mortification. John fled to the kitchen for towels and a broom as Suzette stooped to pick up flowers. She kept her eyes on the floor and avoided looking at either of his parents.

Fortunately, the evening proceeded without any other embarrassing incidents. John and Suzette were introduced to many family friends, who wore the eternal country club uniform of navy-blue blazer, tie, and slacks. Everyone smelled of perfume and cigarettes. Suzette repeated "It's so nice to meet you," too many times to count.

The next morning, John's father headed to the golf course and his mother left for a lunch appointment. Miraculously, they had the house to themselves.

His hand gripped Suzette's waist. "Kiss me." When she leaned over, his other hand went between her legs, teasing her from the outside of her panties. They kissed with tongues twisting, their bodies pressing tightly against each other.

He sat up and tugged at her shirt. "Let's take this off." He unhooked her bra and she dropped her arms, letting it fall to the floor.

His hands roamed everywhere as they explored each other and kissed. They lay tangled together in his room until John heard the garage door going up.

By the time his mother came to check on them, they were fully dressed and sitting with a pile of video tapes scattered between them. As soon as she walked away, John leaned over and kissed Suzette.

"Pretty good timing, I'd say."

His parents played bridge that night and didn't join them for dinner. Instead, John drove Suzette around Vero Beach and stopped at a small bistro with outdoor tables under the stars. When he touched her, it was like an electric current shot through her. She could barely eat her hamburger.

After they drove slowly back to his parents' house, John ignored the front door and walked around to the backyard, stalling for a few more moments of privacy. Past the swimming pool, he pulled her onto a wooden bench built into the dock.

The breeze ruffled his dark curls in the moonlight as they watched sailboats anchored in the Intracoastal Waterway.

"I love your hair," she sighed.

"Take it — it's yours. It's too thick and curly. I love long, straight blonde hair." He tugged on hers.

He pulled her legs across his lap and grabbed her hands.

"You know that I'm in love with you, right?"

Suzette kissed John as though she was trying to merge their entire bodies through their lips. When they broke for air, she looked at her watch.

"Wow, it's eleven o'clock already," she said. "I guess we should hit the sack."

"Is that an invitation?" he teased.

"I'm sure your mother and father would *love* that," Suzette whispered.

With their arms around each other's waist, they reached the sliding glass doors to the house. It was dark inside, apart from a hallway light that his parents left on for their wayward son and his guest. Suzette saw a flash of blue silk pajamas and a woman's bedroom slipper disappear around the corner. She felt a moment of panic, knowing the woman had been spying on them from inside the house.

"*How long was she watching?*" Suzette wondered. "*What was she thinking?*"

John's mother was pleasant enough the following morning as she served them a plate full of exquisite French pastries and freshly squeezed orange juice. Suzette ate carefully and tried not to leave a stain on the linen napkin. After they finished eating, his mother gave John a stiff, almost wooden hug and wished them a safe drive back to the naval academy.

When they arrived at the school, Suzette lingered outside her front door. "I had a wonderful time," she said

"Me, too. Having you there, made staying with my parents tolerable." He sighed. "I hate Sunday nights. I won't see you until after school tomorrow."

Suzette felt her stomach lurch. She hated Sunday nights, too.

EIGHTEEN

uzette enjoyed driving around Sanford. It was a
cute little town and she felt safe, no matter what
street she took, no matter which way she turned,
which was quite different than Boston.

Occasionally, Mom let Suzette drive to Julie's house
after school. "You need some girl time after living with
all these midshipmen."

It was true. Suzette also valued her sensible friend's
advice: *You should know by now that the only person
you can control is yourself.* Learning to accept that she
couldn't control her dad's illness had lifted an incredible
weight off her shoulders.

She spent so many years riding an emotional roller
coaster that it had begun to seem weirdly normal. Often,
she felt very alone . . . living uneasily with a father who
was there; but wasn't.

Julie wanted Suzette to meet her friend, Elizabeth, who
was visiting. "She went to school with me when we lived
in Connecticut," Julie explained.

The girl was petite, with a shiny black bob that perfectly grazed her shoulders. She was a senior this year
and had come to Florida to visit a few colleges. The three
girls sat on the floor around a coffee table in Julie's living
room and shared a pizza.

Glancing at Julie, Elizabeth began talking. "My mom
started to go to Al-Anon meetings to cope with my dad's
drinking. She wanted me to go to a group called Alateen
that's for kids who struggle with alcoholic parents, but
I said no. I really thought I could handle things on
my own."

She twirled a strand of her hair. "I didn't think I needed
any help, but playing the babysitter at home affected my
schoolwork, and my grades started to suffer. The school
counselor strongly suggested that I go to Alateen, as well.

"I guess as Dad's drinking and his moods got worse, I
found myself breaking down more often. I finally went
to my first meeting. Although it felt strange and kind of
uncomfortable at first, I sort of found relief in that room,
listening to people's stories, and the way they dealt with
the alcoholic parent in their lives."

She stared at a spot in the distance. "Knowing that
other people were going through the same thing as I
was, took my mind off my own problems. When I was
there, every Monday night, the things going on at home
couldn't touch me. I could breathe for a while."

There was a comfortable silence as they nibbled on
the pizza.

"Sometimes it's easy to see what alcohol is doing to
the *drinker*," Julie said. "I think it's harder to see what
it's doing to the rest of the family. I mean, the people
who live with a drunk react to his behavior, right? They
probably try to control it or even hide it. But I'm pretty

sure nothing works. At least it didn't with my uncle. Maybe we can find an Alateen group around here?"

"Yeah, I guess I should check it out," Suzette said, thoughtfully. "I don't know what my mom would say, though."

"I learned it's important not to isolate yourself from other people," Elizabeth whispered. "Anyway, this isn't about your mom. This is about *you*."

Suzette remembered the night when her father gripped her shoulder so hard at the dinner table that a bruise swelled. First purple, then a sickly green. She was too embarrassed to explain it to anyone, so she avoided wearing a bathing suit.

"Thanks for the advice. You're right."

In chemistry class at Our Lady of Perpetual Guilt, Suzette partnered with a girl, whose dewy pink face practically glowed. During their freshman year, Suzette distinctly remembered the same girl's complexion was plagued by angry, red acne bumps. As she adjusted her safety goggles, Suzette complimented her lab partner on her skin and asked about the total transformation. She was told it resulted from visits to a dermatologist, along with a magical drug called tetracycline.

Suzette could hardly wait to tell Mom and begged for an appointment. She began following the same skin regimen as her classmate — popping tetracycline pills and hadn't seen a pimple in months. Her skin looked as flawless as a magazine model. Soon, however, she began to notice a persistent itch in an area where polite people weren't supposed to scratch.

"Mom, I think I need to see a doctor," Suzette confessed one afternoon. "I'm really itchy down there, and it's impossible to scratch it in public."

Mom raised an eyebrow. "I'll call and see when I can get you an appointment. I haven't switched detergents or used anything that might give you a rash."

Suzette never minded going to the pediatrician. She wasn't one of those screaming kids who had to be dragged into the examining room for a shot. But this doctor's office was different. Nobody offered her a lollipop or toys to play with in the waiting room. There were just a lot of ladies reading magazines, until they heard their names called.

Mom didn't go with her to the examining room. The nurse asked Suzette to step on a scale to get her weight and measured her height. Then she handed her one of those blue paper "gowns," as they're called and told Suzette to leave it open in the front for the breast exam.

"But my breasts aren't the problem. The itch is lower."

The nurse smiled and read the chart.

"Everything off and then put this over your lap." She handed Suzette another blue paper sheet before she left. The examining room was freezing cold, so Suzette decided to leave her white ankle socks on.

The nurse returned, accompanied by the doctor.

"I know this is your first exam and I'm going to ask you to spread your knees as wide as you can," he instructed. "That goes against everything you've been taught in school, but it will help me with the exam. Scoot your bottom down toward the end of the table and put your feet in the stirrups."

Suzette scooted until she felt like she might slide off the table and into his lap. It was very embarrassing.

The doctor pulled something out of sealed plastic wrap and Suzette watched as he smeared some clear jelly stuff on the end of it.

"I'm going to do the pelvic exam. This is a speculum. I use it to open up your vagina so I can see inside more clearly. It won't hurt, though it may feel a bit uncomfortable. Just relax."

Suddenly she felt the warmth of a bright light shining between her legs. It reminded her of the spotlight on her school stage and she briefly considered belting out a song. Instead, she looked up at the ceiling and felt something scraping inside her. Frightened, she squeezed the nurse's hand tighter.

"All through," the doctor said, turning away and peeling off his surgical gloves. "We'll send this to the lab but I'm fairly certain you have a yeast infection, brought on by the antibiotics you used to clear up your face. It's a fairly common side effect. I'll write a prescription for a cream you'll use at bedtime."

After the nurse and doctor left the room, Suzette used the paper sheet to wipe off the gooey stuff before putting her panties back on. "*Having a few zits might be easier than doing this.*"

NINETEEN

Suzette noticed the atmosphere at the naval academy during spring semester was strained. After worrying about finishing their applications before the deadline, most of the seniors worried about getting into their dream schools. Every guy she encountered grumbled under the stress—some complained of headaches, others had difficulty sleeping, trouble concentrating, or lost their appetite.

"I think it's the lack of control that really makes guys feel crazy," said Big Mac. "Fortunately, I'm not worried about getting into a big, brand-name school. I'm going back to the family business in Connecticut."

Waiting for the last of their college letters, the midshipmen had to deal with rejection or, for the lucky ones, the difficulty of deciding where to spend the next four years.

"I hear the Ivy Leagues and other top-tier institutions only accept around five to six percent of their applicants," someone complained on the Quarterdeck.

To cope, Big Mac told Suzette that some stashed ice from the mess hall in their toilet tanks — along with cans of beer.

"I've even found liquor bottles hidden in stereo speakers," he said, shaking his head. "Those guys spend their time waiting for college news while serving detention."

As graduation neared, college acceptance and rejection letters flooded the academy mailboxes. A lot of guys started freaking out. The Captain reported one midshipman had thrown a plate of pasta at his friend and then stormed out of the mess hall because the friend got accepted to Duke and he had been wait-listed.

During afternoon liberty, midshipmen gathered at the lone pool hall in downtown Sanford. As they racked the balls, they interrogated each other. "Hear from any colleges, yet?"

"If I had, you'd already know."

Big Mac selected a pool cue and waited for another boy to break.

The striped and solid balls scattered across the table, with two dropping into corner pockets.

"What about you?"

"I got into Florida State."

"Congratulations." Big Mac said. "You can relax, now."

Mom noticed tension between the boys, too.

"Even top students need ways to relieve stress," she told Suzette over a cup of tea. "I read in the newspaper that students at the nation's top-ranked law school can check out a loaner dog from the library to help reduce their stress. They say that therapy dog visits bring increased happiness, calmness, and emotional well-being."

"Great, Mom," Suzette said. "Maybe we can send Skipper on a mission of mercy to the guys' dorm rooms upstairs."

"It makes me sad to think these boys don't understand that, after a certain point, getting into a selective school is a matter of luck," Mom mused. "It's not a measure of their character."

Suzette grabbed her cheerleading gear and headed for the gym. The squad usually practiced for two hours after school. Today, one of her knees felt a little stiff, but she hoped the warm-up stretches would take care of it. She still couldn't get down to a complete split, but she jumped higher than the rest of the squad. That was the good news. Girls of all sizes were needed for various stunting positions, so no matter what you excelled at, you were an asset to the team.

When cheerleading practice ended, Suzette noticed John and Gary standing by the bleachers. Gary was grinning and clapped John on the back as she picked up her pom poms.

"Hey, ski queen," he called to Suzette, waving as he left the gym. She fell into step beside John as they headed across First Street to the main academy building.

John cleared his throat.

"My parents called this afternoon and read my acceptance letter from Auburn over the phone. The university sent it to my home address, not here. Looks like I got in."

"Of course, you did," Suzette answered and forced a smile. "They don't get many Battalion Commanders applying, I'll bet. Congratulations and go War Eagle."

A lump lodged in her throat and she couldn't talk anymore. He stared mournfully at his shiny black uniform shoes and she realized the joking part of the conversation had ended. Her stomach lurched as he explained that Gary wanted to be his roommate. The pain felt like an appetizer before the full portion of heartache arrived.

For Suzette, the situation felt eerily familiar. Her years as a military child put her in the position of always leaving or being left. Relationships were short-lived. At the end of each school year, she might leave — not just for the summer, but for good. She learned to deal with the repetitive grief and the loneliness of starting over.

Just never with someone she loved as much as John.

She took a few deep breaths and tried not to think too deeply. She decided to ignore time and pretend the end wasn't coming. She would spend every moment she could with John. He was her anchor and without him, she would be adrift.

Julie said that first loves almost never last.

Suzette was confident . . . or desperate . . . enough to try.

John suggested they focus on planning for the prom and asked if she wanted to eat dinner by themselves.

"Gary really pressured me to join him and his date," John told her. "He was kinda weird about it, but I just kept telling him no."

Relieved, Suzette admitted she didn't want to spend the night talking to Gary's date, whom she had never met.

For weeks she searched for the perfect dress and finally bought a pink halter gown with cutouts on either side of her waist. John rented a rose brocade jacket that complemented it. Mom took millions of pictures and when they got in the car, the fragrance from Suzette's gardenia wrist corsage filled it with an amazing scent. White flowers bloomed practically from her hand to her elbow. It felt good to drive together, to be heading out of their tiny town.

"Well done, Battalion Commander, sir," she said, holding her arm in front of her to admire the flowers.

"As an officer and a gentleman, I must be honest," he replied. "I asked your mom to help me order your corsage. I haven't done it very often and I wanted to be sure that you'd really like it."

"I *love* it," she said, grinning. "And I love *you*."

They chose an elegant, dimly lit restaurant in Orlando known for its romantic atmosphere that the cheerleading coach had suggested. To keep from getting upset, Suzette avoided talking about anything to do with Auburn. Occasionally, that made conversation as stilted and awkward as it had been in their early months together. But the salad and prime rib dinner tasted delicious, the candles were glowing, and John didn't seem to be in a hurry to get back to the ballroom at the naval academy.

"I guess we should go back," he said at last, squeezing her hand. "We still need to have our prom pictures taken before the photographer calls it a night and goes home."

The bill was presented with flourish, in an ornate leather box on a silver tray. John pulled a wad of dollar bills from his pocket, counting them until the stack towered above lid. He self-consciously tried to flatten them before the waiter returned.

"They give us our weekly allowance in singles and I forgot to turn them in for larger bills," he apologized. "I didn't ask my parents for money because I didn't want to tell them about the prom. I was afraid they might arrive for a visit and stare at us all night."

Suzette found the stack of dollar bills totally hilarious. "Thank God," she giggled. "It could be worse, you know. We could have paid with rolls of quarters . . . or dimes."

As they drove to the prom, John's hand reached across and rested on her thigh. It felt perfect or as close to perfect as she could remember—the weight and warmth of John's hand. She laid her hand on top of his, careful not to bruise the gardenias on her wrist, and he spread his fingers so hers could weave in between them.

TWENTY

Suzette was curious when two of the older girls on the cheerleading squad proudly showed off their promise rings, which were smaller and subtler than engagement rings, but still represented love and commitment in their relationships.

With John going off to college in Alabama, she wanted, no *needed*, a tangible symbol of his love.

"All I do when we're apart is think about you and all I do when we're together is worry about you leaving," Suzette blurted out. "I . . . I think wearing your ring might help, but you don't even have a senior class ring to give me."

John laughed and kissed the tip of her nose. "I know, I didn't order one, but I hate wearing anything on my hands. But I bet we could find you something much prettier than a clunky class ring, anyway. And it would fit your finger."

On Friday night as they strolled through a mall, killing time before the movie started, they peered in several jewelry store windows.

Suzette looked at cases full of white and yellow-gold jewelry before she spotted a delicate yellow-gold wedding band with two tiny diamond leaves. It was supposed to curve around a diamond engagement ring, but Suzette thought the design looked beautiful on its own. She pointed to the glass case.

"May I see just the wedding ring, please," Suzette said.

"Of course," the salesman beamed at her. "How very economical to skip the engagement ring."

"Actually, it's just a promise ring," John said, his face reddening.

"I understand," said the salesman. "That's a new and very popular trend with couples headed toward an engagement. When you know that your partner is the right one for you but you aren't quite ready for marriage, a promise ring is also known as a pre-engagement ring."

John picked up the ring and slid it on Suzette's third finger. "For the rest of our lives," he said. "One day after we graduate from college and get jobs, or when it's easier financially, I promise to get you a real engagement ring."

Suzette's eyes filled with tears and she thought her heart might explode right there in the store.

By Monday morning, she could not wipe the smile off her face. She could barely concentrate in her classes at Our Lady of Perpetual Guilt.

"You're almost glowing. I need sunglasses to look at you," Julie observed. "Show me the hand. I don't know why you couldn't tell me about this sooner."

"I was afraid you'd be mad at me," Suzette admitted.

"Sometimes you can be so ridiculous. Is he a good kisser?"

"Do you think I'd be this excited if I promised myself to a guy who wasn't?"

Any girl who attends Catholic school has reservations about premarital sex. Suzette wasn't afraid of going to hell, but she was afraid of getting pregnant or even an STD. She also feared that sex would hurt and she might bleed. And then there was the threat of acquiring a bad reputation. Although she knew lots of girls on the cheerleading squad who were having sex with their boyfriends they didn't seem to be judged too harshly.

Julie looked over Suzette's shoulder and spotted one of the football players watching her. She had a split second to make a decision—look away and pretend she hadn't seen him or smile and offer some meaningful stare that would make him want to get to know her better. She chose the latter.

"What is it about the *chase*," she sighed. "Why am I not supposed to show a guy how much I like him? Like my feelings would be too gross. Instead, I just sit over *here* with you, an arm's reach away, and look off in a different direction. And pretend I'm so distracted *by whatever* that I can't be bothered to notice him. That's when guys seem to want you the most."

Suzette laughed at the absurdity and shook her head. She was glad that her relationship with John had evolved past all that stuff. She still had one class left but found herself already dreading the bus ride home after school. It would be hot, riding for an hour on a sticky, vinyl bus seat. The worst thing was the regulars on the bus already claimed their seats on the first day of school. People who were lucky enough to have a whole seat by themselves definitely didn't want to share it with a girl who lived with 'the Anchor Clankers'.

Some of them slunk down into their seats with their eyes closed. One red-faced boy—Suzette couldn't tell if it was from acne or the heat—sat by himself with his backpack on the seat beside him and looked out the window. Message understood.

Standing at the front of the bus, she spotted an empty seat behind the driver and hurried toward it. She sighed and tugged at her white blouse, which already stuck to her chest from perspiration and looked almost translucent. She didn't have the energy to argue.

When she was with John, Suzette felt special. She lived for those moments, his body pressed against hers and his mouth on hers. All the other hours of the day were spent looking forward to the moments they could be together.

Sitting on a bench facing the lake, John's chin scraped against her forehead. He may have been only eighteen years old, but he was a man: strong, athletic, and masculine. His chest pressed against hers. It was as if he was drawing the very breath out of her with his kisses. She brought her fingers up to his hair and slid them into his curls. She couldn't shake the fear that this was going to end, so she wanted to open her eyes and watch every minute of it.

They loved being near the water, sprawled in the sand at the beach, listening to the roar of the waves and seagulls. Sometimes they would linger at twilight and build a bonfire. They sat in the sand, partly in shadow and party lit by the bonfire glow. *It's always easier to talk in the dark when you can't see the other person's face and you don't worry about how they're reacting to what you say. You can just . . . talk.*

In the days leading up to graduation, everything they did felt like a long goodbye. Suzette was nostalgic for a time that wasn't over yet.

One afternoon, John's arm wrapped around her shoulders so tightly there was almost no space between them. He leaned against her and talked about his older brothers and ancient parents. It had been lonely growing up in a house that felt empty, with a father who spent his days traveling for business or teeing up golf balls. That's another reason why John chose boarding school, but he still lacked companionship. Until he met Suzette.

Suddenly, she didn't know what to do with her eyes or her hands. All the teasing in his voice was gone. "What I'm trying to say is, you're it for me. There's no reason to think we're going to stop loving each other when I go to college. We're going to have a wonderful life together."

She pulled him even closer, then put her arms around his waist.

"I know," she whispered. "I'm not going anywhere, either. You're stuck with me."

On graduation day, Suzette sat beside her mother on a cold metal folding chair in the civic auditorium. She caught her breath when two lines of graduating midshipmen in crisp white uniforms marched into the auditorium as the academy band played "Pomp and Circumstance". She turned and caught Gary staring at her from the line at the rear of the auditorium. He waved. Mom grabbed Suzette's hand when John and Big Mac appeared, side by side. Big Mac smiled and nodded when he caught sight of Mom out of the corner of his eye.

Wearing his dress uniform, the Captain stood next to the headmaster and other dignitaries onstage. The Valedictorian began his speech with the announcement that he had received an appointment to the U.S. Naval Academy in Annapolis. At the other end of the spectrum, Suzette knew the class president was going to work in his family's fishing business. She watched the guest speaker (an admiral with an impressive array of medals on his chest) congratulate the senior class on their achievements. As he gave them tips for their future success, Suzette stifled a yawn.

If she leaned forward in her chair, she could see the back of John and Big Mac's heads several rows ahead of her. They had removed their hats, revealing closely-cropped hair that formed perfectly straight lines just above their collars.

I bet that's the last haircut either of them will have for months. She grinned.

The commencement ended with the lowering of the American flag and dozens of white military hats tossed into the air.

It was time to say goodbye.

John reached them first, with a kiss for Suzette and a hug for her mother. Over his shoulder, Suzette spotted his parents standing with several other adults.

His mother looks so annoyed. Maybe those are his aunts and uncles?

"Mrs. LeBlanc, I'd like you to meet my parents," John said. "These are my two older brothers . . ."

Yikes, they sure are older. His brothers look like they should be his parents, while the Elliotts look like his grandparents. Suzette was shocked.

John's mother's hand felt limp in Suzette's, her greeting as cool as the wind blowing off Lake Monroe.

It wasn't until she had her son's full attention, that John's mother began to smile. His brother's wife pulled Suzette into a family photo and John slipped his right hand around her waist. His left hand gripped the military sword that still dangled from his belt.

Suzette was working hard to keep tears at bay. She felt like she was anchored to sand, waiting for the next wave to hit her. The midshipmen she was closest to — whom she loved — were abandoning her.

They're all leaving me behind.

Eventually, John's father lit his pipe and suggested the family head to lunch.

"I'll call you later," John whispered as he squeezed her hand.

"Okay." Her voice wavered with emotion.

Big Mac towered over the other graduates as he waved Mom and Suzette over. His parents, brothers, and sisters congratulated him and posed for pictures.

"We hope you'll come to Connecticut and visit us," Mrs. McGrath smiled warmly at Mom and gave her a hug.

"Thank you," Mom said. "You know I love your son like one of my own."

Big Mac turned to Suzette and enveloped her in a bear hug. She didn't want to let go.

His chin quivered slightly. "We'll get together. You can come north and maybe we can meet up in New York. I'll show you the city. And I'll visit Florida every winter, I promise."

Tears hovered on Suzette's bottom lid, defying gravity. She nodded.

A ball of emotion lodged itself in her throat and she could barely speak. She heard lots of promises to "get together soon" or "when we're out on break." But she knew from watching the midshipmen who graduated the previous year that those get-togethers probably would never happen. Once those guys scattered across the country, they never looked back.

Suzette felt her mother's arm wrap around her shoulders, steering her toward the Captain. He was standing close to the stage, surrounded by the extended family of a midshipman he had once saved from jail after an incident at a liquor store.

"Sir, we appreciate everything you've done for our son," the father said, shaking hands.

The captain smiled at Catfish and patted his shoulder. "I know how thrilled you must be to see him graduate."

TWENTY-ONE

John told Suzette that the main reason for starting Auburn University in the summer semester was because he couldn't stand the thought of spending June, July, and August with his ancient parents in Vero Beach.

"I can't believe your mom agreed to let you drive to Alabama with me." He grinned.

"More precisely she's letting me drive with you *and Gary*, your roommate, for summer semester," Suzette corrected him. "Mom probably thinks there's safety in numbers."

The morning they left, the three stood in front of the empty naval academy, John's 1967 Impala SS packed with bedding, dishes, and stereo equipment. Suzette briefly worried about leaving her mother home alone with a drunk, but squared her shoulders, took a deep breath and tossed her tote bag into the back seat.

Mom hugged all of them and told them to drive safely. "Call me when you get there, or I'll worry and call the state police."

Gary didn't look thrilled to drive alone in his Camaro, which was equally stuffed with college necessities. Suzette wasn't sure if he could see out of the car's rear window.

The boys opted to live in an apartment off campus. They had enough of dormitory living after four years at the naval academy. When John parked in front of a two-story brick building, Suzette thought it looked like an old motel. Their apartment was on the second floor, so the trio hauled everything up two flights of concrete stairs. It contained few furnishings, including a sofa, a table and four chairs. The single bedroom contained two double beds and a nightstand. It wasn't exactly the Ritz, but it was better than a standard dorm room.

Suzette went with the boys to a freshman welcome orientation on the lawn and noticed lots of parents sitting with their sons and daughters. Probably going away to boarding school left John and Gary's parents less involved than others. After all, their boys hadn't lived at home for the past four years. (She was pretty sure Mom would want to spend the first night in her dorm.) She listened intently to the session on *Life as an Auburn Tiger*, learning about academic programs and services, campus life, and Auburn traditions.

I'm going to like going to college here, next year.

They walked to the grocery store to get cereal, pasta, and eggs, which were easy to fix and easy to eat. When John came home from classes, they kissed until their lips were numb, stopping themselves at the very edge of someday, saying not yet, not here, even though it took willpower that Suzette didn't know she had. All she wanted to do was stay in this safe, easy place with John's arms around her. No parents, no stress and in a perfect world, no roommate like Gary.

One morning after John left for his classes, she washed their cereal bowls in the sink and turned on the television. She heard the shower running and guessed that Gary was getting ready for class, too. Stretched out on the living room couch, she flipped through the local channels to find something other than a game show to watch. When she looked up, Gary stared at her from the doorway with a towel around his waist.

"Must be nice to have nothing to do all day, no classes to go to," he was smiling in a creepy, flirtatious way that made Suzette extremely uncomfortable. "I'm through in the shower, if you want to get in."

Take off my clothes with you in this apartment? Are you kidding?

"Um, no. I'm good. I'm going to take a walk and find the bookstore in just a minute." She grabbed her purse and began rifling through it. "I just want to be sure I have a key to let myself back in after you're gone."

"I can help you look for it," Gary said, perching on the arm of the sofa. The towel opened slightly, revealing his naked thigh. "Maybe you left it in the bedroom."

There was something about the way he said *bedroom* that made the hair on the back of her neck stand up. He was leaning way too close and she began to panic.

"It's okay. I've got it right here." She waved the key as she backed toward the door and tried not to glance down at his towel, which was tied so loosely that it looked as though it might drop to the floor any second. She didn't like the look in his eyes. Every fiber of her being told her to run.

She slammed the door and did just that. Two blocks from the apartment, her breathing slowed and she tried to think clearly about what had just happened. Though

Gary didn't *say* anything specific to her, his actions and expressions were all too obvious.

Why was he coming on to me?

The thought made her slightly nauseous. If she told John about the incident, she was pretty sure it would destroy the relationship between the two roommates. She didn't want to do that since the semester had barely begun and she was going back to Florida. She figured it might be best to keep her uneasiness to herself.

For God's sake, Gary can't be hoping that John and I will break up?

The next few days passed quickly, and Suzette made sure that she was never alone in the apartment with Gary again. She left with John and explored the campus while he studied.

The night before Mom picked her up on the way home from a visit to Boston, Suzette and John walked to a diner downtown. They sat at the counter and Suzette watched the stainless-steel wheel above the kitchen spin. White order slips clipped to it looked like a laundry day for garden gnomes. John stared into the bottom of his plastic cup and swirled the dregs of his drink with his straw. He was quiet for a long time.

"I want to be with you all the time," he finally said. "You're the smartest and the funniest girl I've ever met, and I can barely get through the day knowing you'll be so far away in Sanford. I can't help myself. And what if some Catholic-school guy starts looking good and you don't want me anymore?"

"Not gonna happen," she sighed and kissed him. He trailed kisses up her jawline to her ear. Her breath was quickening. John felt safe, warm, and familiar. She could hardly wait to get back to his apartment and curl up next to him on the couch. Hopefully, Gary would have a night class.

Her mother greeted both John and Gary with hugs when she arrived in Auburn. She asked questions about their classes and the campus before looking at her watch. "We'd better get on the road. It's a long drive back to Florida."

Suzette had barely closed the car door when the barrage of questions began.

"How did you like the university?" Mom asked.

"It's very big." Suzette stared out of the window, counting every mile marker on the highway with a despairing kind of dread. Florida seemed so far and, without John, she felt empty inside.

"Did you have time to visit the mass communications department? You know, ask anyone about classes in your major?"

Mom, please shut up. The sound of her mother's voice left her feeling irrationally annoyed. Suzette closed her eyes. "I'm really tired."

She feigned sleep and hoped her mother would give up on conversation.

"I know you're miserable over leaving John at college," Mom said. "And I know you've heard that "hometown honeys" usually bite the dust during the first semester. But John is a sweet boy and I don't think that will happen. He spent most nights this past year sitting at our dinner table. He and Big Mac felt like part of our family and I miss having them around every day, too."

Suzette was afraid her mother would never stop talking. *My family probably saw more of him this past year than his own parents did. I wonder how people could send their kid off to boarding school. I'd miss him so much.*

Mom babbled on. "I'm sure John would never hurt you intentionally, but circumstances change. He's only eighteen years old, on a big college campus with lots of other girls."

Suzette said nothing, so Mom turned the car radio on low and continued.

"I met your father when I was twenty— just four years older than you are right now. It was so exciting to date a navy pilot during the war. Then he would leave on a mission and . . . well, I understand how it feels to be left behind. I just wish I could think of something to make you feel better."

Suzette knew all she could do is wait.

TWENTY-TWO

Suzette feared a summer without John would be boring. She hadn't planned on hurricane season.

They got home to find the Captain standing in front of the television set, listening to a news guy drone, "Potential impacts of the hurricane include hazardous winds, life-threatening flooding, rainfall across Florida, and high surfs along the south and southeast facing shorelines."

A hurricane was predicted to bring winds of 150 mph or above, according to the National Weather Service. Such strong winds meant it was likely to cause catastrophic damage.

"We may need to evacuate," the Captain said tersely. "The school superintendent told me that many people in town already have filled sandbags, boarded up their homes and lined up to buy gas before leaving. We may have a day or two to prepare, but other situations might call for an immediate evacuation. Planning ahead is vital to ensure that we can leave quickly and safely, no matter what the circumstances."

He turned to Mom. "I want to keep a full tank of gas in the car in case we need to evacuate quickly. Gas stations may be closed and unable to pump gas during power outages. We'll only take one car to reduce congestion and delay."

"Where would we go?" Suzette asked.

"We'd probably head inland and away from the coast. I hear sometimes it's hard to find a place to stay that will accept pets. Most public shelters allow only service animals."

Suzette picked up her dog. "We're not leaving Skipper."

"Of course not," the Captain said. "We need to put together a family emergency kit with a battery-powered radio and extra batteries. The authorities say we should have a three-day supply of water (1 gallon per person, per day) and nonperishable food like tuna fish, along with a manual can opener."

"We've never owned an electric can opener," Mom said, looking distracted.

Suzette carried Skipper to her room and laid her on the bed. "I wish John was here," she whispered to the dog. She also wanted something else to arrive—her period.

She pulled the small paper calendar she kept in her nightstand out and stared at the dates. Her period should have started a week ago, but nothing happened. No pimples to announce its imminent arrival, no backaches or cramps . . . nothing.

She took a few deep breaths. *I know we didn't actually have sex, which is usually necessary to get pregnant. But what if some stuff was on his hands when he touched me, there? Could I still get pregnant?*

Anxious to block the thought from her mind, she walked to the kitchen, opened a cabinet and pulled out a first-aid kit. Mom rifled through a drawer and found a flashlight with extra batteries.

"I also want to keep an emergency blanket, a wrench or pliers, duct tape, and a pair of work gloves in the trunk of our car," the Captain added. "Could you put our important documents and emergency numbers in a waterproof zip lock bag? We also need our prescription medications and pet supplies for Skipper."

Mom turned to look at the television just in time to hear the meteorologist warn, "Follow recommended evacuation routes. Do not take shortcuts; they may be blocked. Be alert for road hazards such as washed-out roads or bridges and downed power lines. Do not drive into flooded areas."

The governor appeared next, saying widespread power outages and other problems would follow the storm. Suzette watched forecasters warn that spinoff tornadoes could also be a threat.

A tornado would certainly take care of my problem. My parents would kill me if I had a baby. They'd probably want to kill John, too. How could I go to college? Do they let you bring a baby to class?

She turned back to the television and tried to focus. The city encouraged residents to shelter in place or stay with family or friends in homes outside of these hazard areas that were designed, built, or renovated to withstand hurricane conditions. Authorities cautioned that storm surge and rain were the cause of most direct deaths from hurricanes. Since 1963, ninety percent of deaths occurred in water-related incidents, mostly drowning.

Maintenance men at the academy already cut plywood to cover school windows and added extra security to keep the doors from blowing open. They tried to secure the historic building from damaging winds.

"It all starts with the roof," the Captain said, looking up. "The roof is the largest potential opening on the building. I'm told that wind and water can do terrible things if they get through the roof."

"At least it would flood the midshipmen's rooms on the two floors above us before it reached our apartment," Suzette said to Mom.

The old stucco building had survived many storms in the past, but there were audible creaks from its timbers. The wind suddenly strengthened and with it came the rain. Liquid fingers of water crept under the front door as Mom wedged a bath towel on the floor. Somewhere in the building there was a heavy thud and a crash.

"I'm going to check the upper floors. I'll take the maintenance man with me," the Captain announced.

The good news about a hurricane is he doesn't have time to drink.

Water surged over the lawn and frothy waves lapped at the front steps. The street beyond it looked like a canal. Skipper began shaking—she always hated thunder storms. During a flash of lightening, Suzette thought she saw the outline of an oak tree laying on its side. She had never minded storms in the past and thought the brilliance of lightning flashes was often beautiful. Just not tonight, when Mother Nature appeared to be having a temper tantrum, tearing the landscape apart.

When he returned, the Captain reported a set of entrance doors had blown open.

"The rain is coming down with such force it feels like needles stabbing your skin," he said, water dripping from the brim of his cap. Mom handed him a towel.

Windows rattled, as though some demon was trying to shake the glass from the frames. Suzette peered outside through a crack in the plywood that had been used to board up her bedroom window. She gasped when she saw palm trees starting to bend and crackle in the wind. Sheets of rain spattered the glass and she thought it sounded as if someone was flinging handfuls of marbles at it. A red roof tile sailed past and the air seemed to be alive with pieces of wood and metal that became a barrage of missiles.

If the school collapses, I won't need to worry about being pregnant. I may not survive. Anyway, it's not technically possible. Ask any health education teacher. It would be a miracle if I have a baby.

She had been checking her underwear throughout the day, each time hopeful. As if sensing her panic, the building trembled and Suzette thought the rain blew horizontally past it. Those wind gusts could knock a person off their feet. She listened to the storm hissing through the stucco, as if testing it, looking for a way inside.

It howled so loudly that Suzette had to practically shout at her mom just to be heard. The television news showed footage of crazy fools surfing the giant swells off the beach. She curled up on her bed with Skipper under her arm, away from any window that might shatter and cover her in glass. Impossibly, she fell asleep.

Suzette woke later feeling a little groggy. She could hear a faint noise from the television down the hall as she yawned and stretched.

"Where's your mother?" her father asked, suddenly appearing in the doorway.

"I don't know," she mumbled, rubbing her eyes. "I just woke up."

He nodded and Suzette noticed that his face was flushed. He sat down heavily and began scratching Skipper, who was lying on the bed beside her.

"Awww, she's a little ticklish on her paws today," he slurred cheerfully.

Suzette glanced over and saw the dog struggle to get away from him. When the dog jumped down from the bed and scurried from the room, the Captain grabbed Suzette's foot instead.

"What are you doing? No, Dad, stop it. That hurts."

Her father had a sickening grin on his face and his eyelids drooped in the familiar way that Suzette had grown to hate.

"Stop it. Get out."

One of his hands gripped her ankle while the other dug into the sole of her foot, in his drunken attempt to tickle it.

"Stop it. Get out of my room."

Suzette was screaming now. She tried to kick him with her free leg to get him to loosen his grip but even drunk, the Captain was strong. She grabbed hold of the headboard and tried to pull her body away as her mother hurried into the room and began laughing loudly. Suzette stared at her mother, horrified. Had everyone in the house gone crazy? This wasn't funny, this hurt.

"GET OUT. GET OUT. Mom, get him out of here."

Mom's eyes grew wide as she stopped laughing and started pleading.

"Come on, Paul. Stop it. She doesn't like being tickled. Enough is enough."

He wasn't listening, just grinning idiotically and digging his fingers deeper into Suzette's foot.

"Paul, please. Stop it, now. Go watch television. That's enough."

The Captain slid off the bed onto the floor and sat, dazed, for a moment. He abruptly stood up and shuffled back to his leather recliner in front of the television.

"Are you alright?" Mom looked frantic.

Suzette nodded and wiped her eyes. Slowly, her heart stopped pounding.

I can't wait to move out of here. John would never do something like that. Living with him would be calm and . . . safe.

The sky outside remained a battleship-gray color. Within twenty-four hours the rains ended, the clouds had broken, and weather conditions cleared. If not for the damage, debris, and flooding left behind, Suzette would never guess that a massive storm had passed through. She stood with Skipper in the quiet left by the wind and noticed the complete absence of birds. No gulls, no herons, no egrets, or sparrows. The school grounds were an empty wasteland.

The sun burned through a hole in the clouds and though the hurricane was gone, they were about to face a new disaster—mosquitoes.

"The groundskeeper says when there is a deluge of rain, a deluge of mosquitoes is sure to follow." The Captain's face looked grim, but sober at the breakfast table.

The newspaper reported the Seminole County mosquito control staff sprayed insecticide in anticipation of a mosquito outbreak after intense rainfall.

"The worst part isn't just the bites that make us itch like crazy," Mom reached for the sugar bowl. "Mosquitoes also spread viruses like encephalitis. Remember when we drove behind a truck spraying great clouds of poison? That kills the insects while they're still in the larvae stage.

"I think the county mosquito control also has airplanes out spraying for mosquitoes before they grow into adults," Mom explained. "They clear ditches with standing water and I read that they stock ponds with minnows because the fish feast on mosquitoes. Talk about the circle of life."

The Captain announced he would drain water from garbage cans, buckets, the pool cover, flower pots or any other containers where rain water might collect to minimize the risk of disease. "I need the staff to get rid of old tires, drums, or anything else that might hold water outside."

Suzette was relieved to hear the door close behind him.

"Honey, before I forget to tell you, the groundskeeper warned me that we've all got to wear shoes, socks, long pants and shirts with long sleeves." Mom stirred her oatmeal. "He said we should put mosquito repellent on our bare skin *and* our clothes when we take Skipper out for her walks. I've got some bug spray with DEET around here, somewhere."

She looked at a ripped screen outside the apartment window and shook her head. "Those have got to be repaired fast. We don't want any mosquitoes getting inside the house."

Back in her bedroom, Suzette noticed some papers in her purse. Pulling them out, she saw a brochure titled *Alcoholics Anonymous*, and started reading.

> "Alcoholics often take out their hostilities on others in irrational ways and may not be able to express love appropriately. Those of us who live in alcoholic situations may act irrationally as well."

Duh, no kidding.

> "Experts do not agree on exactly what makes a person an alcoholic. However, since alcoholism does tend to run in families, the children of alcoholics are at greater risk. Learning about alcohol, and its effects, can help us to make a decision about its place in our lives."

Great news. I can grow up to be just like him.

Suzette remembered strolling past a rack of information pamphlets while she waited for her prescription from the dermatologist to be filled at the pharmacy. She must have dropped one into her purse when her name was called.

She didn't really have a relationship with her father. He wasn't home much when she was a little girl because he flew planes off aircraft carriers. According to her mother, "The Navy will always come first." Not surprisingly, as a teenager, Suzette responded to his rare attempts at affection by stiffening or moving away from him. Those attempts felt foreign and intrusive, reminding her of what was missing and, at least at first, what she used to hope for. Over the years, she built a great wall against wanting any of that from him anymore. It was too late. The wall was impenetrable. She felt safe behind it.

Suzette woke the next morning with horrible cramps. Bright red drops of blood splashed in the toilet bowl. At the sink she rinsed out her underwear until the water went from red, to pink, to clear. She flicked the light switch and looked in the mirror at her hair, a mess from sleep, that barely concealed a new zit on her forehead. She draped her panties on the towel rack and took a Midol. She had never been more grateful to feel so awful.

Suzette was still shaken from the tickling incident when she met Julie at the mall a few days later. She needed some distraction and figured shopping — combined with a hot fudge sundae — would do the trick.

"You have to remember that an alcoholic is sick, so he hurts himself and others," Julie said. "When you live with one, you develop problems, too. You can't help it. My uncle lived with us for a while. He was kind of a wild one in high school who turned into a real problem drinker by the time he got to college. My family learned the best way to help a compulsive drinker, and ourselves, is to build our own strength, be kind, and learn how to detach from the problem."

"Easier said than done," Suzette muttered, rolling her eyes. "I just want to move out."

"Yeah, well, my uncle doesn't live with us anymore. I guess my mom was afraid he was a bad influence on my brother, sister, and me. She read some statistics from a National Study on Drug Use and Health survey that said thirty-five percent of high school seniors have five or more drinks in a row at least once in a two-week period. That led to weeks of listening to discussions about her worst nightmare — drunk driving."

"I just don't get binge drinking," Suzette said. "I mean, do you even taste anything if you're just trying to get wasted? I must be some kind of control freak, because I like to know where I am and what I'm doing most of the time."

"No, you're not," Julie said, grinning. "I get lectured all the time, 'It's important to always be aware of your surroundings and who you're with.' I'm not even sure where people get stuff. Our Lady of Perpetual Guilt has drug prevention policies so strict that we can't even offer an aspirin to another student on school property, much less a beer or a joint."

They stopped at a cosmetics counter, where Suzette picked up a perfume bottle and sprayed a paper square.

"Take a whiff and tell me what you think."

They thumbed through racks of T-shirts and bell-bottom jeans—"civvies" that could never be worn to classes at a parochial school.

"Do you ever get tired of not fitting in at school," Suzette asked, "of always standing on the outside, looking at the popular girls' cliques?"

Julie paused. "Sometimes it's just important to persevere, even if the situation isn't exactly what we want it to be. I'm okay with the superficial friendships that don't exist once school is out for the day. I've always been the odd girl out. I was the one who came from somewhere other than a school down the road. I hope when we get to college, things will be different. Or I'll be so busy with premed classes, I won't notice."

"You're really going to be a doctor, huh?" Suzette asked. "Not an option, for me. I could never pass the chemistry classes. You're the whiz kid."

Julie laughed. "I'm sure you could pass premed chemistry if you really wanted to. Do you have any idea what you'll major in?"

She pulled Suzette in the direction of the ice cream shop.

"Yeah, I think I do. I wound up taking journalism as an elective last year and worked on the school newspaper. It sounds weird, but I really enjoyed putting little pieces of information together in a story that makes sense. It's like putting together pieces of a puzzle, when you interview several sources."

"It's not as weird as cutting into a human body," said Julie, pointing to a gallon of Rocky Road ice cream in the case. "I'm not sure I want to be a surgeon, anyway. But if I find a cure for cancer, you can interview me and write about it. Then, we'll both be famous."

TWENTY-THREE

Suzette spent Saturday afternoon running errands with her mother. When they arrived home, they were surprised to see John's parents sitting on the living room couch. The Captain sat in an armchair across from them, holding a letter and Suzette was aware of the silence. It was a different sort of quiet—uncomfortable and icy. The kind that means not only that no one's talking, but that something very specific is not being said.

The Captain handed the letter to Mom as she slid into another chair. Suzette glanced over her mother's shoulder and read the opening:

"Dear Mr. and Mrs. Elliott,

Suzette sensed something awful was about to happen and turned her eyes — both hopeful and terrified at the same time — toward John's parents.

There was no warmth emanating from the couch at all. They might as well have been sitting on a block of ice. A crease between Mrs. Elliott's brows was deeper than Suzette had ever seen it. As she looked at the older woman, Suzette realized what a mix of confidence and entitlement looked like.

"Mrs. LeBlanc, we are shocked that you would let your underage daughter stay with our son without an adult present,"

John's father said, his eyes blazing.

"Did you not consider the ramifications? Do you not care about your daughter's reputation? Or my son's, for that matter?"

Suzette winced. It was painful to hear them turn an innocent trip into something ugly. Technically, much of it was true. But their son didn't have sex with her. Why couldn't his parents see it was Gary's jealousy that prompted the letter they received?

Mom said simply that she loved and trusted both John and her own daughter completely. She knew how much the kids missed each other. The Captain's jaw was set and his expression, blank, revealing nothing.

"Sir, we didn't do anything wrong," Suzette protested, her cheeks burning.

Mr. Elliott shook his head, then turned and glared at her. "Young lady, you must end this with John immediately."

"But I can't," she said, faintly. It didn't sound like her voice.

"Then let me inform you, we shall stop paying our son's tuition at Auburn and bring him home to live with us in Vero Beach immediately. We'll give him time to reevaluate his priorities and you will *not* be welcome to visit." Mr. Elliott's chin jutted out belligerently.

Suzette's mind raced. She was pretty sure that her parents couldn't afford to send *both* she and John to college and the thought terrified her. She couldn't be responsible for something like that. She had never seen people *look* as hateful as the Elliotts did, with their cold and ugly expressions. She hoped that she never would again. Even their posture exuded anger. They refused to look at her.

This can't be real. I must be hearing them wrong.

The situation was completely blown out of proportion, like some funhouse mirror or the Salvatore Dali painting that John loved. It was incomprehensible.

This. Isn't. Happening.

When the Elliotts stood to leave, it was as if all the air got sucked out of the room. Suzette watched her father walk them to the door. Her mother remained in a chair, visibly flushed and on the verge of tears. Suzette was breathing hard by then and for a few seconds, that and the pounding in her head were the only things she could hear.

"What . . .," she finally said when she was able to speak again. "What is going to happen, now?"

Mom rubbed her temples and closed her eyes. "I wish I knew."

Suzette didn't want to deal with the Captain, so she headed down the hall to her room. She just wanted to be with John, in some other life, loving each other. Everything felt so right when they were together. Her eyes were swollen and her throat ached from crying. Suzette wondered if it would ever go away, the wrenching feeling in her stomach that came whenever she thought about a life without John.

She berated herself for remaining silent with his parents. Why didn't she *say* something to convince them they were wrong? Why didn't she *do* something? Sitting politely wasn't exactly the best solution to the problem — they didn't *deserve* politeness. They were *rude*. But their angry presence made her feel as if she had been paralyzed. Now, it was too late. Her silence had a cost.

John called a few hours later.

"I'm so sorry," he said, miserably. "I just heard from my parents about their trip to see you. They arrived at my apartment two days ago and surprised me, too. They didn't call, they just showed up and handed me a letter.

> *"Dear Mr. and Mrs. Elliott, You don't know me, but my little brother rooms with your son at Auburn University. I am writing to let you know how difficult it is for him work on his studies when Suzette LeBlanc stays in the boys' apartment . . ."*

Suzette thought she might have to drop the phone and run to the bathroom to vomit.

"Gary left for a visit home on the exact weekend my folks came to Auburn to confront me," he said bitterly. "My dark side thinks he disappeared at a convenient time. He knew exactly what was coming.

"When he got back to our apartment on Sunday night, he knew that I was mad and conflicted about something," John continued. "I'd like to know why his sister would write a letter like that to my parents. I'm trying to give him the benefit of the doubt, thinking your visit just slipped out during a conversation with his sister. I mean, he never expressed any jealousy to *me* about my relationship with you."

John paused for breath.

"I guess one time I did tell him that my relationship with *you* trumped my friendship with *him*," he said slowly. "I honestly don't know if that sparked his anger or revenge. I guess, in hind-sight, our conversation might have been the catalyst for him telling his sister about your visits."

"After I handed the letter back to my parents, I tried to make them understand why your mother had trust in *me*, in *us*, and that just added more fuel to their shock," he added, miserably.

"They probably resent the fact that you were close to my Mom," Suzette murmured.

"I had no idea they planned to drive to Sanford to see you and your parents," he said, his voice cracking a bit.

"It was horrible," Suzette cried. "Your *parents* were horrible. Your father was a bully. Mom was so embarrassed, and I just wanted to die. What are we going to do? They're threatening to stop paying your tuition."

"I'll fix this," John promised. "I'll get student loans. If I can't, I'll drop out and get a job. I can finish college later, after we're married. I swear I'll figure out how to deal with this mess. Please tell your mom and dad that I apologize for my parents. I wish they would just stay out of my life and leave us alone."

After he hung up, Suzette dozed out of sheer exhaustion and woke up with a gasp, her heart pounding in her chest as if she had been chased. Her eyes were stuck shut and swollen from crying and her face had been pressed hard into the pillow, leaving a roadmap of red lines down her cheek that looked slightly sinister. There was a part of her that regretted the messy girl in the mirror, but another part relished her appearance because it matched the way she felt inside.

Skipper was a good listener when Suzette needed to unload. And the dog could be counted on for unconditional love any time of the day or night.

"My life is a mess," she whispered, absently scratching the dog's ears.

Skipper tilted her head, probably trying to pick out words she knew like, "cookie" and "treat." She gave her standard contribution to any conversation: a lick on Suzette's cheek.

Awake for most of the night, Suzette looked up at the man in the moon outside her window. She heard her mother open the bedroom door to check on her and pretended to be asleep. She didn't have the physical or emotional strength to discuss it anymore. She was glad to hear Mom's footsteps fading down the hall.

Suzette stared at the black and white picture of John she kept in a frame on her nightstand. He was in uniform, leaning against a tree and looking away from the camera. She loved having it be the first thing she saw when she opened her eyes in the morning and the last thing she saw before she fell asleep at night. "*Thinking of you*" he had written across the bottom. She ran her finger across his smiling face beneath the glass and tried to separate the disastrous events in her mind. What, exactly, lead to this war with his parents? It was as confusing as trying to find the beginning and end of a strand of spaghetti in a bowl. If she hadn't . . . then . . . maybe his parents . . . wouldn't . . .

She tried to remember the way that she and John used to be. The memories her brain conjured up were always the same: Driving home from the beach with the windows rolled down, his suntanned chest above faded denim cutoffs, driving one-handed with the other holding hers. She smiled, knowing all those images would stay with her forever. Yet the hole in the hull was too big for their little ship to sail on. She could not let him throw away his college education for her.

When John kissed her, it totally transformed her world. It was like the first time she put in her contact lenses, everything just came into focus.

She overheard her mother whispering "heartbroken" into the phone. She thought it sounded melodramatic and yet, still so insufficient.

Mopey and sullen, Suzette focused on small tasks, like cleaning her sink. In fact, the more depressed she felt, the more her bathroom sparkled. Rejection by John's parents deeply wounded her and proved that some choices were simply beyond her control. *They wouldn't actually stop paying his tuition just to prove a point, would they? What kind of parents could be so cruel just because their son loves a girl?*

The future terrified Suzette. Despite her best efforts, life might not turn out the way she wanted.

Mom finally gave up on trying to talk about the situation. Suzette was alone, just like she hoped, and it felt terrible.

"I miss him so much," she whispered to Skipper. The loss snuck up on her, black and cavernous.

The next day, she went to cheerleading practice, though she no longer cared much about the rest of the girls on the squad or the routines. She didn't want to talk to anyone, or explain anything, so she left as soon as practice ended. Walking back to the apartment, she stopped and plucked a rose from the bushes in front of the academy. Its petals quickly turned brown and wilted after she plopped the flower in a vase of water.

There's a great metaphor for my life. That rose looks exactly the way I feel. She felt something inside herself curl up and shrivel in the same way when she answered the ringing phone in her kitchen. It was John.

"Hi," she said and then her jaw froze. A hundred things to say flashed through her mind, but none of them sounded right. So, she said nothing. The distance between them felt insurmountable. Once she thought talking might make it easier, so why was she tongue-tied?

John rambled about married student housing that was available at Auburn.

"I'm going to check it out today after class," he said. "It should be cheaper than paying for room and board in the dorms. We can buy our own food and cook at home. I don't like the cafeteria meals anyway."

"Sounds good," Suzette said, trying to sound hopeful. "I wish my parents had enough money to send us both to college. But they don't, John. I'm sorry."

"Don't worry. I love you and I'll find a way out of this. I'll fix it. I promise."

TWENTY-FOUR

Days were dismal, classes bored her, and she couldn't seem to concentrate. Everything—and everyone—was annoying. That's why Suzette did what she always did when she needed comfort and distraction.

She headed for the library.

In junior high, she loved visiting old public libraries in Boston, with their stained-glass windows, massive marble columns, amazing ceiling designs, and wonderful polished woodwork. They must have been expensive to build, but she figured that the compelling beauty of the building ought to inspire everyone who walked through the doors.

In addition to the architecture, Suzette loved the *smell* of a library: More than the smell of paper, it was the smell of adventure and far-off worlds. It was the smell of a million words, each a door to somewhere new. And the place was blissfully *quiet*. People couldn't talk to you without the disapproving glare of a librarian. In other words, it was perfect.

Of course, Our Lady of Perpetual Guilt had a relatively small library. But it still offered long wooden library tables and chairs where you could hunker down and hide. It would have to do.

She stared at rows of books lining the shelves and wondered if John would ever forgive her . . . if he would ever understand that she couldn't let him throw away his future. *We can't always control our circumstances, who our parents are, where we live or how much money we make. But there are rare moments when we can shape our fate, when we do have the power to make our own decisions. We just can't be too scared to make the tough choices.*

Julie slid into the empty chair beside her. "What is going on with you? I couldn't tell if you were in class or in a coma."

Suzette looked up to be sure the librarian was in her office. She closed her eyes and whispered a short version of the visit from John's parents.

Julie's eyes widened with every word. "Holy shit."

She listened until Suzette's voice began to falter and she choked back tears. Then Julie reached over and squeezed her friend's hand. "Don't worry. It's impossible to let go of the people we love. Pieces of them stay embedded inside us, like splinters, I guess. And we think the pain will kill us, but it won't. Eventually, scar tissue forms around those pieces and they don't hurt as much."

Tears ran down Suzette's cheeks. "How'd you get so smart?"

Julie looked down. "I listen a lot and from what I've heard, I think our first love affects our lives forever."

The girls walked through the hallways at Our Lady of Perpetual Guilt, which were buzzing about the upcoming Sadie Hawkins Dance. Posters hung on every open wall and the dance committee hawked tickets outside the cafeteria during lunch.

"For some idiotic reason, a lot of girls have decided to wear the same or *extremely* similar clothes, in order to match their dates," Suzette observed.

Julie shook her head. "Unbelievable. You can tell who your date is because he's wearing matching clothes. Suppose *he* looks better in the outfit than *you* do? So, are you going to ask John to drive down for this fashion disaster?"

"I guess so. I mean, it's a Friday night and I'm not sure about his class schedule. I'll check with him and see."

"Good. But if John can't make it and I don't find a date, we can go together. I don't mind wearing a matching outfit with *you*. We can be twins."

Suzette laughed, in spite of herself. Later that night, she finished her Spanish homework, snapped the book shut and called John. He picked up on the second ring.

"How's it going," she asked softly.

He sounded tired. "A bit overwhelming, actually. I try to do most of my work in the library, since I can't stand the sight of Gary. I'd like to beat him to a pulp. I don't spend much time in the apartment, just enough to shower and sleep. He stays out of my way."

Suzette guessed the boys' friendship ended after the incident with John's parents. The ripple effect just kept growing and it hurt her to see John's life was still full of aggravation. "Can't you find a new roommate?"

"I could if we lived in a dorm. Unfortunately, both of our names are on the apartment lease. I'm hoping he flunks out and doesn't come back after Christmas."

"You're such an optimist." Suzette smiled into the phone. "I wanted to check with you about going to a Sadie Hawkins dance at my school. Your parents don't need to know about it. There'll be lots of hay bales and I'll even buy us dinner."

When he heard the date, John groaned. "That's in the middle of mid-term exams and I've got a major project for my art history class due, which I haven't even started yet."

"Oh, that's okay. It's no big deal. Just thought I'd ask."

"Why in the world do they call it a Sadie Hawkins Dance?" John asked in a puzzled voice.

"Didn't you read the Li'l Abner comic strip? Sadie Hawkins Day was when the unmarried women of Dogpatch got to chase bachelors and marry the ones they caught. Now it's just a dance, where the girls get to invite the guys instead of vice versa."

"Well, I admit I kind of like the idea of being asked," he chuckled. "Takes the pressure off for guys. You have no idea how hard it is to work up the courage to invite a girl out and be turned down."

"You're right, I don't," she teased. "And *you'll* never have to worry about it again."

He was silent for a moment. "Look, if you really want to go to this, I'll figure out a way to get my stuff done. I don't sleep much these days, so maybe at night . . ."

She interrupted. "Don't be an idiot. It's a dumb dance. They move the tables out of the cafeteria, hire a DJ, and charge everyone twenty-five dollars to occasionally dance. Most kids just huddle in groups, spreading rumors. It doesn't matter if we go."

He stifled a yawn. "Okay. But I don't want you to be disappointed."

"No worries." Yet deep down, she was.

Suzette ignored the chatter about the dance, the endless wardrobe debates that raged between couples in the hallways after classes. Instead, she focused on planning John's birthday. In a few weeks, he would drive down from Auburn to celebrate with her.

"*I bought you a present you can hold in your hand and think of me*," she wrote in a letter. As she licked the envelope, she glanced at the expensive set of art pencils on her dresser. There had been a dizzying array at the art supply store, but the salesman assured her that these were the best pencils out there. Wrapping them carefully in navy blue paper printed with white anchors, she gingerly wound strands of ribbon around a scissors and curled each one until the package looked perfect.

She re-read a note he enclosed in his card, *I can't wait to see you*, and smiled.

"I think I'll bake his favorite carrot cake with cream cheese frosting."

Mom was folding laundry on the table. "Good, because I love that one, too. Do you know what time he'll get here?"

"No, not yet. He may leave Friday night after classes or early on Saturday morning. He'll call me to let me know for sure."

"It will be good to see him again," Mom said. "There are fresh sheets on the bed in the guest room, so it will be ready whenever he arrives. Do his parents know he's coming? We don't need to cause any more problems, Sweetie."

Suzette shook her head. "He didn't tell them, and I don't care. If they were *normal* people, he could talk to them."

With a visit from John to look forward to, the days passed quicker and though classes were still boring, they were tolerable.

"I'm happy to see that your mood has improved," Julie murmured sliding into a desk beside Suzette. "I was worried about you."

"Yeah, John will be here next weekend for his birthday," she said, happily. "We'll have two whole days to talk without his creepy roommate or his parents."

"Sounds perfect," Julie said. "You deserve it."

Knowing that John was coming lifted Suzette's anxiety. They could talk face-to-face and figure out how to handle his family. When Friday finally arrived, she could hardly wait to get home.

His present rested on the guest room bed, along with the mushy birthday card she signed with Xs and Os. On the nightstand, Suzette added a yellow rose in a vase that she bought at the grocery store. *Just like the ones he sent me for my birthday.*

She had just walked back into her own bedroom when the phone rang. It was John.

"I just came home from class and found my parents sitting in my apartment." He sounded upset and gloomy. "They drove to Auburn to surprise me for my birthday."

What?

"Ahh, what are you going to do?" Suzette tried to stop her voice from shaking as much as her shoulders.

"What *can* I do? I can't leave here and admit I'm going to see *you* just yet. I pretended that I had to get something out of my car and now I'm standing at the pay phone across the street. I didn't invite them, I swear. I haven't spoken to them in *weeks*."

"I know, I know." Suzette struggled to keep from crying. "They ruin everything. I just . . . wanted to see you on your birthday."

It sounded so lame, but she couldn't hide her disappointment.

"I'll make it up to you, I promise. I just don't want to fight with my parents again. It seems like all we do is argue these days. I love you, Suzette. I'll call as soon as I get rid of them."

She hung up, wiped her eyes and realized no amount of planning or apologizing was going to make this situation better.

After plans for John's birthday weekend fizzled, Suzette's irritation and despair hung in the air like bad perfume. She gave up trying to read and closed each book, lethargic with grief. She slept for days with the blinds closed and the curtains drawn. Each time Skipper demanded that Suzette step into the daylight to go for a walk, she thought she might go blind.

Talking to John might help, but between her class schedule and his, she could never be sure when to catch him at home. She certainly didn't want to speak with Gary if he picked up the phone. *I couldn't even be civil to that creep.*

She started to write several letters but didn't know what to say. Nothing had changed. There was no good news to share. If his parents had changed their mind, she felt certain he would call. When she answered the phone one night and heard his voice, her heart began to beat faster. Maybe he had some *good* news?

But the sadness in his greeting told Suzette everything she needed to know. His parents' anger was irreparable.

"I'm pretty sure I can get student loans. We don't need my parents' money." She heard the desperation in his voice, the same as she read it in his letters. She closed her bedroom door and slid down to the floor with her back against it.

"John, this ugly situation with your parents is never going to work out." She hung her head as the words tumbled out. "I don't want you worried about money when you should be worried about your college classes. It would be way too much pressure to cope with. We'd both have to work a bunch of jobs and we'd probably wind up flunking out. Don't you see the impossibility of *us*?"

A sharp stone of loss seemed to settle in her throat, so big that it made it hard for her to breathe.

She closed her eyes and tried to empty her mind of the sight of her own parents' faces as they listened to the Elliotts. Her stomach lurched and swallowing became a struggle. How could she marry into a family that hated her? She and John would live like starving outlaws, estranged from everyone. And if he had to drop out of college to work, eventually he would hate her, too.

John pleaded with her not to break up. He mailed several letters back to her, ones that she had written to him early in the summer, proclaiming her love. If his intent was to jog her memory about their relationship, it didn't have the desired effect. The letters only made her remember the disdain on his mother's face as she sat in Suzette's living room. Her look made Suzette feel like the whore of Babylon and her opinion would never change.

She and John were being torn apart and she would be left alone in an unremarkable, ordinary life in high school without him. Overwhelmed with guilt and sadness, Suzette couldn't continue dragging John down. Because she did love him and she realized she would never be accepted by his family. She loved him too much to ruin his life.

Mom was waiting at the dining room table for her. "Can I get you an aspirin?"

Suzette shook her head. She could find no painkiller to blunt the edge of things, to alleviate the chronic, aching torment of her memory.

She ate without tasting anything. To appease her mother, she ate even though she wasn't hungry. She couldn't muster a smile, too emotionally exhausted to even make eye contact with her mother much less rehash everything. But when she finally did look up from her chair, she didn't see judgement in her mother's face. Instead, she saw sympathy.

"I hope I did the right thing," Suzette said in a quavering voice. "For him and for me . . . for both of us."

Mom patted her hand and spoke quietly. "I miss John, too, Sweetie. I know it's only a fraction of how you must be feeling, but I thought you might want to know that someone else is thinking about John."

Suzette nodded. She didn't know what else to do.

One Saturday, she woke to the hum of a lawnmower and the aroma of freshly mowed grass. As she lay in bed, staring at the ceiling, she discovered an important thing about herself: Her magical ability to overlook what she didn't want to deal with, to put painful memories out of her mind and never think about them again.

If I pretend that awful event doesn't bother me, after a while it actually won't.

Every Psychology 101 student knows that it's not the event itself but how you *respond* that tells the story. Expose a dozen people to the same life crisis and they will react differently. Suzette realized that she was the girl who will try to never think of it again.

But the cost was high — the dwindling of her spirit, the resignation that replaced her enthusiasm, the cynicism that eliminated her hope.

I guess the slate will never entirely be wiped clean. The experience with John's parents was a total disaster, but it will live in my past and affect my present, no matter what I try to do about it.

When she thought about her first trip to Auburn, she saw how they were in danger. Not because of the circumstances, but because they were innocent and didn't even know it. They believed that the future was theirs and they could take time getting there. Suzette never considered that anything could go wrong. She never considered the power of a disgruntled roommate and controlling parents.

Now, it was as if all the color had gone from the world and even sounds were muffled as if she was swimming underwater. Her world would be a different place without John in it and that fact made her feel unbelievably tired.

One morning when she was unable to sleep, Suzette shuffled out of her bedroom to find the apartment quiet. Pools of sunlight filled the wooden floors. She poked her head around the kitchen door and found it empty. Mom wasn't there. Her socks snagged splinters on the old wooden floorboards as she turned on the kettle. She plopped a teabag into a cup followed by two pieces of bread into the toaster. When they popped up, she slathered them with butter, cut them into triangles and settled at the table. Her nana always made tea and toast for her. It was kind of comforting to eat it as she looked out the window. It had been almost one hundred days that she had woken up without John in her life. She began to consider the possibility that somehow, incredibly, she could live without him.

I can always join the convent.

Some days she slipped outside to walk along Lake Monroe when Sanford was wrapped in in the pearl gray of dawn. After a couple of hours, the sun emerged like a dazzling debutante, charming everyone who looked at it.

Suzette looked at the enormous palm trees beside the lake. Their intricate, spindly trunks were a testament to their resilience against the hurricane-force winds that battered them. She turned away from the water and looked up at the naval academy that had been her home for the past two years. Standing in the middle of the grassy lawn holding Skipper's leash, she brushed a few annoying ants off her bare foot. Gradually, a sense of calmness settled over her that soothed her soul. Even though it was only a few months since John's parents delivered their ultimatum, when she thought about that day it no longer felt like part of her life. It seemed more like a bad movie.

She began to consider the possibility that there might be a dim light at the end of this tunnel and she might just be okay, eventually. She would just have to keep getting out of bed each day and putting one foot in front of the other. Like all good sailors must.

There's no way his family will ever like me or accept me. I won't make him choose between us. She, too, had a choice to make — to recover or exist in a miserable state forever. It was time to move forward in a different direction.

TWENTY-FIVE

Temperatures sizzled in the nineties by the time Suzette dropped her books on the bed and spotted a stamped envelope on top of her pillow. She stared at her name, written in John's narrow, slanted cursive, trying not to let the sight of a small square of folded paper undo her.

She didn't really even want to touch it. She felt the pain radiating from inside the envelope. Yet, she couldn't help torturing herself by reading and re-reading his letter. He asked if she was okay, if he could visit. He wondered if she was angry at him, if they could talk. On and on, the paper held a series of pleas that seized her with guilt. John wrote of marriage plans that she no longer intended to keep. Her loneliness, bottomless and black, rushed in. *What happened has happened. It's over.*

Halfway through his letter she stopped reading. Those memories were way too sad. She wasn't that girl anymore. She didn't want to go back and revisit the pain, so she stopped writing back to John. She guessed that everyone had a heartbreak in their life at some point.

What happened didn't make her weird or unusual. It was simply part of being human.

After all, how many books have been written about broken hearts—starting with Romeo and Juliet?

She clutched Skipper as if she were drowning and the dog was her life preserver. She missed John, and in that moment, she missed him with her whole body, aching for the future they thought would be shared . . . the one they were ordered to abandon.

Suzette looked down at the dog and felt as if Skipper was asking for news. *He's gone*, she wanted to say, but she didn't because she didn't trust her voice, and because it sounded totally ridiculous anyway.

Suzette opened the front door one Saturday evening and was shocked to see John standing on the other side.

"I came all the way here so that when I talked, you'd *have* to answer me. All of my calls and messages have been through your mom. Do you have any idea how many times I tried to reach you? I started to feel like a stalker."

His eyes teared up and he laughed bitterly.

"Of course, you know. Because you got all my letters and my message,s and you decided not to respond."

"I . . . I . . . didn't know what to say," she stammered.

John was angry. She could see it in his shoulders and the way he wouldn't look her in the eye. She closed the door behind them and walked to the seawall across the street with him. They stood looking out on Lake Monroe, invisible and alone. Side by side, they couldn't even see each other. Lights twinkled at a hotel and marina across the lake.

People must be ordering dinner, talking to each other about their day. Suzette felt the distance between them and the rest of the normal world grow larger.

"Maybe you can tell me why you came to the decision to avoid me. I've been wondering exactly what I did to bring about that reaction."

"What happened with your parents . . . it was uglier than you can imagine," she says. "My parents were mortified, and I was embarrassed, too."

Words were so difficult.

"They *hate* the thought of me with you," Suzette said. "And I hate *them*, but we can't fix this. They're old and idiotic, but they're still your parents. You need them and their money."

Although he was angry, he was still John. Kind and fiercely loyal, he found her gaze and smiled that soft, adoring smile. Even though it summoned every shred of strength left in her body, she could see the truth: this has to end.

She counted every second he was next to her with a despairing kind of dread. He asked her to go for a ride and for a few minutes, it felt familiar. They drove through a fast-food restaurant and ordered drinks. John's hand reached across and rested on her thigh. It was warm, like the cup of hot chocolate she held tightly in both hands.

He pulled into a parking space, shut the Impala engine off and turned to face her.

"What's going on?" he asked, shaking his head. "Don't you still love me? Why are you acting this way? We have to fight them . . . fight for our future. I don't get it."

A sob was building at the base of Suzette's throat. Now the sob burst from her. "I can't."

She buried her face in John's chest and began to cry. "This is a battle that we won't win."

She was afraid to look at him, afraid of the feelings that would surface if she did. He rested his chin on top of her head and held her hand, his thumb running over the promise ring.

"I'm glad to see that you're still wearing this. Suzette, I *am* angry, but not at *you*. I'm sorry if I made you think that."

Neither one spoke. Suzette could feel a headache starting to pulse and wondered if she had made a huge mistake in honoring his parents' demand.

I can't do this.

John sat silently, as though reality had finally sunk in.

"All right," he said, pressing the heels of his hands into his eyes. "If that's the way you feel, I guess I won't change your mind. I can't believe you're giving up on us."

A tear slid down Suzette's cheek.

"I love you," she whispered, but she knew the words sounded like good-bye.

TWENTY-SIX

A ttendance at daily mass in the Our Lady of
Perpetual Guilt chapel was better than going
to class, but not by much. Suzette didn't mind
receiving the Communion wafer on her tongue, but
she always passed on sipping wine from the goblet. She
didn't think a quick wipe with a linen cloth eliminated
viruses. And she didn't want to end up like the Captain,
who used to be an altar boy.

"The Catholic church probably didn't know about
germs and diseases when they started the tradition," Julie
observed. "I don't like sharing a cup with tons of other
people, either."

The pair left the church during the final hymn, walking
slowly along a dirt path through fragrant pine trees back
to the classroom building.

Suzette hated boring her friend with all of the sordid
details, but sometimes she felt if she didn't talk about it,
her head — and her heart — might burst.

"Does everyone feel this way when they lose someone, like their life is completely undone? When I look at my face in a mirror, it isn't mine anymore."

Julie dutifully listened and shook her head. "You can't make people love you. Love isn't something you earn, like extra credit. Anyway, there are more important things than being loved by John's creepy old parents."

She leaned forward in the library chair.

"Like being of service to others. With love, you're waiting for someone *to give* it to you, you know? But service is something *you* give. And you don't give it just to people you care about. In fact, it's better if you serve people you don't even *know*. You can serve *anyone*."

Suzette wiped her eyes. "Is that why you sit here and listen to me weep and wail?"

"You need me, so I listen," Julie said with a shrug. "I don't know, when I help someone, it's like I'm helping myself, too."

"That sounds terribly Catholic. Don't let Sister Mary Margaret hear you or she'll sign you up for the order." Suzette laughed.

"When something awful happens, you've got to do things that make you feel good. Being active, making things better in whatever way I can — that makes me feel good. Not particularly religious, just *good*."

"Thank you for being an amazing, supportive friend," Suzette said. "I promise I'll listen whenever you need to vent about something, and I'll love you forever. Of course, that's assuming that I live through this and get over John."

"You can." Julie paused and cleared her throat. "And you will."

She waited a minute before she continued.

"I've been wanting to talk to you about something, but you've been pretty upset and I never found a good time. I guess there never is a really good time."

She ran a hand through her hair and tucked it behind her ear.

"I've decided to skip my senior year and go to college, instead."

Suzette blinked.

"I've got years of medical school ahead of me and I just can't fathom wasting another year at Our Lady of Perpetual Guilt," Julie blurted.

"How can you do this?" Suzette asked slowly.

"Florida Tech will consider applications from exceptionally qualified high school students who want to enter college after their junior year," Julie answered. "Students interested in this kind of early admission typically have outstanding high school records and have exhausted the educational opportunities available to them at their high schools."

She winked at Suzette. "I'd say that we both qualify."

"We have to get decent SAT scores, of course, and write some pretty amazing essays. But Florida Tech offers early admission, assuming that your GPA is satisfactory. And I'm ready to move on."

Suzette's stomach churned. Julie knew her so well. She had seen Suzette at her best and worst. They had reached the point in their friendship where they could be quiet together and it wasn't awkward. Or they could sing along with the car radio very loudly and not be embarrassed. Suzette had lost John and soon she would lose her best friend, too. Life was about to get much worse.

That night, Suzette pulled the telephone book out of the kitchen drawer. She flipped through its pages until she found Florida Technological University, which had more listings and phone numbers than coffee grounds in a can. *Academic Advising, Admissions*, and finally, *Office of the Registrar.*

She called the next day and was told, "We provide information about registration, academic records, and degrees. This office uses the latest technology and procedures to enhance student, administrative, and faculty services. Would you like to schedule an appointment?"

Suzette hung up and found her mother sitting at the kitchen table. Mom looked up, her green eyes sparkling, but Suzette knew they would cloud over when she heard of the plan.

Mom listened to the Early Admission program details and twirled the pen in her hand. "I can't tell you what to do," she said finally. "It's your decision."

Suzette rolled her eyes. "You've been telling me what to do since I was born. Why stop now?"

A week later, Mom drove to the Florida Tech campus while Suzette acted as navigator and searched for visitor parking signs. They entered a contemporary brick building that felt a lot like entering a refrigerator. In her thin cotton dress, Suzette couldn't stop shivering and she hoped the school registrar wouldn't think it was nerves. They were ushered into the office of a nice man with kind eyes and without much hair.

"The Early Admission Program targets high school students who seem ready, both academically and in personal maturity, to undertake college work," he said looking from Suzette to Mom.

"It's really not a new idea," he continued with a smile. "Prior to the twentieth century, admission to most American colleges was by an exam or by a preparatory course prescribed specifically for that college. Students who could demonstrate their readiness for higher education were able to enter at whatever age was appropriate. Many colleges routinely admitted students as young as fourteen. Some students entered college entirely self-taught, or after having received only informal tutoring. In 1971, Julian Stanley at Johns Hopkins University reignited interest in early entrance with his Study of Mathematically Precocious Youth, in which he worked one-on-one with students entering Johns Hopkins as young as thirteen."

"Wow," Suzette blurted out. "I'll be seventeen, so I guess I'll be fine."

The women left carrying a large envelope filled with forms to be completed and returned. Suzette would sign up for the SAT tests the next time they were offered, but that meant getting registration information from the office secretary at Our Lady of Perpetual Guilt. She didn't really want to discuss her decision to leave high school a year early. She was moving forward, at last.

One of the guidance counselors approached Suzette between classes, as she sat on a concrete bench under the pine trees on campus.

"Hi, Suzette. I just wanted to be sure that you knew that we have scholarships available for our students, if that helps. We don't want you to leave Our Lady because of a financial hardship."

He was young — probably not much older than her own sister and he was trying to be helpful.

"Um, thanks. But money is not really the issue."

She felt tongue-tied. How could she tell him she was leaving the school because she was bored? Because every course she took (other than math) seemed easy? Because the kids in her class felt like younger siblings and she needed new friends, new challenges? Because she already had been invited to John's senior prom and didn't care about waiting around another year to attend her own? Because she wanted to burn her gray pleated skirt and white ankle socks and wear normal clothes again? Because John, the love of her life, was gone and she needed *action* rather than *distraction*?

Suzette's hands trembled slightly so she gripped her notebooks harder.

The guidance counselor waited, expecting Suzette to speak. When she didn't, he shoved his hands in his pockets and smiled. "Well, let me know if there's anything I can do for you."

Suzette nodded and stood up, praying she could make it to the girls' room before she burst into tears.

The following day, she registered for the SAT exams. She drove alone and watched groups of girlfriends whispering anxiously before they were admitted to the testing site. She guessed they would probably go to lunch afterwards and talk about the exams or how they thought they scored.

Suzette sighed. *Alone, again. Nothing changes.*

Several of the kids in the class ahead of her at Our Lady of Perpetual Guilt looked at her oddly when she walked in.

They're wondering what I'm doing here. I'm too young.

Within weeks an envelope arrived from the College Board with her SAT results: 1490 out of 1600. Suzette had proved she was ready for college. More importantly, she was ready to leave high school problems and relationships behind. If she was ever going to be happy again, she needed to focus on a far bigger picture.

Mom beamed when she read Suzette's test scores. "Honey, I'm so proud of you. I knew you were smart enough to go to college. We have to call your sister in Boston and tell her."

Even the Captain smiled when his wife shared Suzette's news. "I expected nothing less from you. Congratulations on a fine academic performance." He then proceeded to celebrate the only way he knew how: He poured himself a drink.

As he walked to his recliner, he stopped and turned to face his daughter. "I'm very proud of you."

"Thanks."

They both fell silent. Small talk was never their specialty.

She hesitated before asking, "Will you and Mom be okay when I leave for college?"

The Captain inhaled, ready to double down on her for insubordination to a superior officer. Then, as if under the guidance of some patron saint of parenthood, he exhaled calmly before he spoke.

"I know sometimes I have too much to drink. I'm working on it. I know it's not a quick fix, but I'm trying."

"That's good, but you might need help, Dad."

It caught him off guard and he stared at her.

"Okay," he said, lowering his eyes to his glass. "I'll think about it."

Suzette heard her mother in the kitchen, silencing the whistling tea kettle, as she walked slowly to her room. *I hope Mom will be okay when I leave. But I can't fix this—fix them—even if I stay home. It's not my responsibility. It's her choice to stay with an alcoholic. Not mine.*

She felt a smile form on her face, muscles that hadn't moved in that manner since John's parents stormed out of her house. She looked down at the promise ring on her third finger. She still loved it . . . still loved John. Slowly, she slid it over her knuckle and held it for a minute. Then she opened the pink velvet box it came in and tucked the slender gold band inside. Its tiny diamond leaves sparkled, winking at her, just before she closed the lid. She placed it carefully in the top drawer of her bureau, beside her grandmother's pansy handkerchief and a miniature sewing machine saved from her childhood dollhouse.

All my treasures are safe and sound. I may even have room for one or two more.

ABOUT THE AUTHOR

Renee Garrison was a newspaper reporter for The Tampa Tribune. During the decade she worked as the architecture critic, she won two communication awards from the American Institute of Architects.

Renee discovered her love of journalism while writing for her high school newspaper and graduated from the University of South Florida with a degree in Mass Communications. This book is a sequel to *The Anchor Clankers*, which won a Gold Medal in the Florida Authors and Publishers Association President's Book Awards and chronicles Renee's life as the only girl living in a boys' military boarding school, The Sanford Naval Academy. Both books are considered "auto-fiction," or autobiographical fiction, which is simply fiction based in your own life experience, but with some loosening of the reins on what "really happened".

Renee grew up with a father who abused alcohol, yet it wasn't until after college she realized the impact his drinking had on her. During bookstore and book club visits, many readers of her first book confided they, too, had an alcoholic parent. Like Renee, they shared these traits:

- Do you constantly seek approval and affirmation?
- Do you fail to recognize your accomplishments?
- Do you fear criticism? Do you overextend yourself?
- Do you have a need for perfection?
- Are you uneasy when your life is going smoothly, continually anticipating problems?

Renee decided to write about the issue in the hope that it might help others who are struggling. As a teen, she wishes she'd known that while she couldn't control her parent's drinking, she could talk about it. And she should have.

Alcoholism is a family problem, and those who live with an addict need to be heard and helped.

For more information and to stay in touch with Renee visit her home on the web at www.reneegarrison.com where you can view her other works, purchase additional copies, and stay abreast of news and upcoming events.

Do you want even more?

Renee invites you to connect with her on her social media channels and to read her blog.

anchorclankers   /author/show/8380640.Renee_Garrison   @reneewrites

Blog: reneewritesnow.wordpress.com